Praise for the first Gilded Age Mystery
Still Life with Murder

"What a thoroughly charming book! A beautiful combination of entertaining characters, minute historical research, and a powerful evocation of time and place. I'm very glad there will be more to come." —*New York Times* bestselling author Barbara Hambly

"Utterly absorbing. Vividly alive characters in a setting so clearly portrayed that one could step right into it. A very clever plot in which each clue is clearly offered and yet the identity of the murderer is a complete surprise." —Roberta Gellis

"*Still Life With Murder* is a skillfully written story of intrigue and murder set during Boston's famous Gilded Age. Nell Sweeney, governess and part-time nurse, is a winning heroine gifted with common sense, grit, and an underlying poignancy. With its rich sense of place and time and a crisp, intelligent plot, readers will speed through this tale and be clamoring for more." —Earlene Fowler, bestselling author of *De____able ____untains*

"P. B. Ryan captures an authentic flavor ____ ____ ____ston as she explores that city's dark unde____ ____ ____ ____ ____er-effects of the war. The atmosphe____ ____ ____ ____ ____ty Irish nursemaid Nell Swee____ ____ ____ ____st. I look forward to seeing he____ ____ ____s Bowen

"P. B. Ryan makes a stun____ ____ ____ge With Murder, bringing nineteenth centu____ ____ from its teeming slums to the mansions on B____ ____tion, and populating it with a vivid and memorable ca____ ____haracters. The fascinating heroine, Nell Sweeney, immediately engages the reader and I couldn't put the book down until I discovered the truth along with her. I can't wait for the next installment." —Victoria Thompson, author of *Murder on Lenox Hill*

"Spunky . . . Readers will admire [Nell] and won't be able to resist her many charms. *Still Life with Murder* is a well-constructed and fascinating mystery in what looks to be a great series." —*Midwest Book Review*

MURDER ON
BLACK FRIDAY

P. B. RYAN

BERKLEY PRIME CRIME, NEW YORK

THE BERKLEY PUBLISHING GROUP
Published by the Penguin Group
Penguin Group (USA) Inc.
375 Hudson Street, New York, New York 10014, USA
Penguin Group (Canada), 90 Eglinton Avenue East, Suite 700, Toronto, Ontario M4P 2Y3, Canada
(a division of Pearson Penguin Canada Inc.)
Penguin Books Ltd., 80 Strand, London WC2R 0RL, England
Penguin Group Ireland, 25 St. Stephen's Green, Dublin 2, Ireland (a division of Penguin Books Ltd.)
Penguin Group (Australia), 250 Camberwell Road, Camberwell, Victoria 3124, Australia
(a division of Pearson Australia Group Pty. Ltd.)
Penguin Books India Pvt. Ltd., 11 Community Centre, Panchsheel Park, New Delhi—110 017, India
Penguin Group (NZ), Cnr. Airborne and Rosedale Roads, Albany, Auckland 1310, New Zealand
(a division of Pearson New Zealand Ltd.)
Penguin Books (South Africa) (Pty.) Ltd., 24 Sturdee Avenue, Rosebank, Johannesburg 2196, South
Africa

Penguin Books Ltd., Registered Offices: 80 Strand, London WC2R 0RL, England

MURDER ON BLACK FRIDAY

A Berkley Prime Crime Book / published by arrangement with the author

PRINTING HISTORY
Berkley Prime Crime mass-market edition / November 2005

Copyright © 2005 by Patricia Ryan.
Cover art by Mary Ann Lasher.
Cover design by Rita Frangie.
Interior text design by Kristin del Rosario.

ISBN: 0-425-20688-2

BERKLEY® PRIME CRIME
Berkley Prime Crime Books are published by The Berkley Publishing Group,
a division of Penguin Group (USA) Inc.,
375 Hudson Street, New York, New York 10014.
BERKLEY PRIME CRIME and the BERKLEY PRIME CRIME design are trademarks belonging to
Penguin Group (USA) Inc.

PRINTED IN THE UNITED STATES OF AMERICA

10 9 8 7 6 5 4 3 2 1

Author's Note

I N 1869, gold was the most heavily traded market on Wall Street. About $25 millions' worth circulated privately in the United States, with more than $75 million held by the federal government.

In April of that year, speculator Jay Gould launched an ambitious scheme to corner the gold market. The idea was to buy up the nation's private supply so that he could sell it for paper currency at his own price, thereby reaping a colossal profit. The only fly in the ointment was President Grant. If he were to get nervous about the rising price of gold, he could drive it back down by releasing some of the government's supply, thereby foiling Gould's plan.

Gould's coconspirators included colorful financier "Big Jim" Fisk and Grant's own brother-in-law, Abel Corbin. There's even been speculation that the United

States Treasury Secretary, George S. Boutwell, was involved. The players were ready; the stage was set.

Gold started soaring in value on September 23rd, which was when Gould, tipped off that Grant was on to him, quietly sold off his own holdings for an estimated $50–$100 million. At 11:00 on the morning of Friday, September 24th, with the Gold Exchange in pandemonium, Grant ordered $4 million in federal gold to be sold the following day. Secretary Boutwell cabled the New York treasurer with this information shortly after noon, but curiously, some investors seemed to know about it already, because the price of gold had started diving at 11:50.

"Possibly no avalanche ever swept with more terrible violence," stated the *New York Herald.* "As the bells of Trinity pealed forth the hour of noon, the gold on the indicator [a clocklike gauge at the Exchange] stood at 160. Just a moment later, and before the echoes died away, gold fell to 138." Within fifteen minutes, it had plummeted to $133 an ounce, inciting a nationwide financial panic.

The stock market reeled. Trading houses went bankrupt. Countless investors were ruined.

Chapter 1

September 25, 1869: Boston

"ARE you expecting someone, Mrs. Hewitt?" Nell Sweeney scooped up a spatula full of warm glue and spread it on the freshly stretched canvas propped on her easel.

"A bit early in the morning for callers, I should think." Wheeling her Merlin chair away from her work in progress, a still life of autumn fruit, Viola Hewitt rummaged amid the paint tubes and turpentine-soaked rags on her worktable. "Where in Hades did I put that watch?"

"I'll get it, Nana." Little Gracie Hewitt leapt up from the solarium's slate floor, on which she had been chalking the shifting patterns of sunlight streaming in through the tall, leaded glass windows. Plucking the diamond-encrusted pocket watch out of the clutter on the table, she clicked it open and offered it to Viola.

Nell, ever the governess, said, "Can you read the time yourself, Gracie?"

Gracie studied the watch intently.

"Where's the little hand?" Nell asked as she ran the spatula down the drum-tight linen, skimming off the surplus glue.

"At the eight."

"And the big hand?"

"At the thwee."

"Three," Nell gently corrected; they'd been working on her diction. "So that would mean it's . . ."

"Eight, um . . ." Gracie screwed up her face in concentration. "Thirty?"

"Eight-fifteen," Nell said.

"Good try, though," Viola said in her throaty, British-inflected voice as she mixed a dab of ultramarine into the rose madder on her palette. "Nell, dear, what makes you think I'd be expecting someone at this hour? I'm not at home for callers till ten—and I'm hardly dressed for company." Like Nell, she wore a gray, paint-spattered smocked tunic over her morning dress.

"Someone knocked at the front door," Nell said as she dipped her spatula back in the glue pot, which was snugged into a pan of hot water. "You didn't hear it?"

"My ears are only there for show nowadays," Viola said as footsteps shuffled toward them along the long, marble-floored central hall.

Hodges, the Hewitts' elderly butler, appeared in the open doorway looking oddly hesitant. "So sorry to interrupt, Mrs. Hewitt. Your son is here to see you."

"Harry? Really?" Viola's roguish and dissolute middle son had spent the past year and a half in self-imposed exile from the family's Tremont Street mansion. As far as Nell knew, Viola hadn't even seen him since June, when his engagement to Cecilia Pratt was announced over dinner at her parents' home. Of Viola's three living sons, twenty-two-year-old Martin was the only one still at home—and the only one who still enjoyed cordial relations with his parents.

Hodges said, "It's not Mr. Harry, ma'am. It's . . . Dr. Hewitt. William."

"Will?" Viola gaped at Hodges, and then at Nell, who shared her astonishment.

It had been almost six years since the Hewitts' eldest son had set foot in this house. Even during his youth, Will had been more of an occasional visitor than a member of the family, having been shunted off to England when he was Gracie's age to be reared by indifferent relatives and educated in a succession of boarding schools—thus inaugurating three decades of semi-estrangement from Viola and her husband. Will's coolness toward his mother had begun to thaw a bit this past spring, before the Hewitts and their staff left for their summer home on Cape Cod, and Will for Europe. As for the stern and venerable August Hewitt, Nell doubted he and Will would ever exchange a civil word again.

Nell listened to Will's approaching footsteps as she buttered the canvas with glue and scraped away the excess, thinking she would have known his unhurried, long-legged stride anywhere. She tried to draw a deep breath, but her stays hindered that, which made her feel like a ninny for wearing so many pointless layers of clothing under this blasted smock frock that hid everything anyway, making her look like some great, fat, ugly, repulsive farmwife. It didn't help that her hastily coiled chignon was held in place with two paint-crusted filbert brushes.

The footsteps stopped.

Nell turned, spatula dripping, to find Will standing just outside the doorway in a handsome black morning coat and fawn trousers, top hat in hand, inky hair smartly combed, smiling at her. She'd seen him just twice since she'd been back from the Cape, all too briefly both times. In the past, he would sometimes join Nell and Gracie for their afternoon outings in the Common and Public Garden—when he was in Boston, and not off playing faro and poker for outrageous stakes in some exotic and dangerous city. But now that he was teaching, he had a good deal less free time during the day.

"Mother." He bowed to Viola, straightening only partially as he ducked into the sun-washed solarium. "What a remarkable display of industry for so early in the morning."

"Almost unseemly, I know," Viola said.

"My thoughts precisely."

Every time Nell saw Will and his mother together, she was struck by their similarities, not just in appearance—the height, the dramatic coloring—but in their manner of speech. Although Will's accent was stronger than that of Viola, who'd spent the past thirty-two years in Boston, they both spoke with the refined nuances of the British upper classes. Even when Will had been an embittered, soul-weary opium addict, he'd always sounded like a gentleman—and usually acted like one, too, despite his best efforts to turn his back on the "hollow, gold-plated world" he'd been born into.

"Nell." He bowed, smiling that coolly intimate smile that he never seemed to use with anyone else.

"Good to see you, Will."

"Uncle Will!" Wiping her chalky hands on her pinafore—a thoughtful gesture that wouldn't have occurred to her just a few months ago—Gracie launched herself into Will's arms.

He groaned with mock effort as he lifted her high, taking care not to let her head bump the ceiling. "By Jove, you're taller every time I see you—a raven-haired beanpole, just like your nana." To Viola, he said, "She's the spitting image of you."

Gracie made an exaggeratedly bemused face, as if "Uncle Will" had said something ludicrous. "Nana's not my weal mommy. She picked me out special 'cause she always wanted a little girl, and she never had one, but now she has me. I'm dopted, wight, Nana?"

"*Adopted.* Yes, that's right, darling." Viola met her son's eyes for a weighty moment before looking away to set her palette on the worktable.

Will, suddenly sobered, kissed the child's forehead and set her down. "I knew that. I was just teasing."

He glanced at Nell, who offered a weak smile as she knelt to wipe up the glue that had dripped onto the floor from her neglected spatula. Setting his hat aside, Will hitched up his trousers and crouched down, a bit stiffly because of the old bullet wound in his leg. "Here." He took the rag from her hand and set about cleaning up the mess himself. "Watching you scrub a floor is like seeing a lovely little mourning dove on a trash heap."

Having always thought of mourning doves as gray and ordinary, Nell wasn't entirely sure how to take that.

"Uncle Will, guess what?" Gracie asked excitedly. "Tomowwow's my birthday, and the next day I get to go on a twain and a steamship."

"You do?"

"The twain goes to, um . . ." The child looked to her nana for a prompt.

"Bristol, Rhode Island," Viola said.

"Bwistol, Wode Island, only it's not weally an island, and then we get on a steamship called the *Pwovidence* that looks like a palace inside."

"The *Providence,* eh? You're going to New York, then, I take it?"

Viola said, "Your father and I are taking Gracie on a birthday visit to your Great-Aunt Hewitt in Gramercy Park. We'll be gone a week."

"Really?" There was a note of genuine surprise in Will's response, and Nell knew why. August Hewitt had never made any secret of the fact that he found Gracie's presence in his home as vexing as that of the upstart Irish governess entrusted with her care. On his instructions, the child took all her meals, except for holiday dinners, with Nell in the third-floor nursery, and he never spent very long in the same room with Gracie before ordering her removed. For him to consent to a weeklong trip with the child was remarkable.

Viola said, "Aunt Hewitt commanded us to visit when she found out Gracie was turning five. She wrote and said she was afraid she'd die without ever having met her. I wrote back that I was more than willing, that it was your father she had to convince. She sent him a letter. I didn't read it, but that evening over supper, he suggested the trip. We're bringing Nurse Parrish along to look after Gracie."

"Nurse Parrish?" Will said dubiously. "She must be ninety by now. Can she still travel?"

"She's eighty-three, and she tells me she's looking forward to the trip. She loves New York, and she hasn't been there in years."

Taking Nell along would, of course, have been out of the question. Mr. Hewitt loathed her as deeply as he did Will. It was only his indulgent love for his wife, and Viola's own steely resolve, that had permitted Nell to remain with the family as long as she had.

"You must draw pictures of the things you see in New York," Will told Gracie, "so that you can show them to me when you get back. I know you like to draw, like Nana and Miss Sweeney." Pointing to the crude but oddly cheerful design chalked onto the floor amid the forest of easels, Will said, "This is your handiwork, is it not?"

"Uh-huh."

"Yes, sir," Nell softly corrected.

"Yes, sir," Gracie echoed. "I dwew the morning sunshine, 'cause Miseeney says she misses it when it goes away."

"How very thoughtful of you." Will awkwardly gained his feet as Gracie resumed her drawing.

"And how very thoughtful of *you*," his mother told him, "to pay a call at the house. You don't know what it means to me, Will. Your, uh, your father is at his office, by the way, so . . ." She glanced at Gracie, who was sprawled on the floor again, chalk in hand. "You know. You needn't worry that there will be any . . . unpleasantness."

"He's working?" Will asked. "On a Saturday?"

"He's worse than ever," Viola said with a slightly weary smile. "Six days a week, he's at India Wharf by dawn." August Hewitt's dedication to the shipping empire founded by his great-great-grandfather was legendary among his fellow "codfish aristocrats."

"I wish I could claim that my visit was prompted by mere thoughtfulness," Will said. "The fact is, I've something rather distressing to report."

"Oh, dear." Viola's smile waned. "I can't say I'm eager for any more bad news, after that frightful gold business yesterday. Your father knows men who lost their entire . . ." Looking up sharply, she said, "*You're* all right, aren't you, Will? You didn't—"

"Good Lord, no. I've never invested in gold." Will kept his considerable gambling swag in the weather-beaten alligator satchel Viola had gifted him with upon his graduation from medical school at the University of Edinburgh. "No. I came through yesterday quite unscathed, but as you've pointed out, the same can't be said for everyone." He looked around, rubbing his neck. "I say, are there any chairs in this room, or—"

"Here." Nell pulled out a paint-speckled kitchen chair that had been tucked under a table. "It's safe to sit on. The paint's dry."

Will sat and crossed his legs, lifting the bad one over the good one with his hands. "Nell must have told you I accepted a position as adjunct professor at Harvard—just for

8

the autumn term. I'm really not cut out for the academic life anymore, but Isaac Foster talked me into it, and it affords me the opportunity to do some rather diverting research. Did you know Foster was named assistant dean of the medical school over the summer?"

Viola nodded. "Winnie Pratt told me about that—crowed about it—when she wrote to announce Dr. Foster's engagement to her daughter Emily while I was on the Cape."

"I'm teaching medical jurisprudence," Will said. "What Professor Cuthbert at Edinburgh used to call forensic studies—the legal applications of medicine. One of my conditions when I accepted the position was the right to conduct postmortems on any good corpses that end up in the morgue at Massachusetts General."

"Good corpses?" Viola said dubiously.

Nell glanced at Gracie, but she was too preoccupied by her artwork to pay any attention to their conversation. Will cast a little half-smile toward Nell, as if to say, *You understand.*

"There are especially interesting corpses," said Nell, who'd assisted at some truly fascinating autopsies during the four years in which she'd been trained in nursing by Dr. Greaves before coming to work for the Hewitts. "Someone whose death was violent or unexplained can be fascinating to dissect, if one knows what to look for."

"I thought the county coroners handled that sort of thing," Viola said.

"Yes," Will said, "but they're all laymen, so they have to pay private surgeons to perform the actual autopsies—when they bother with them. I'm saving them a bit of trouble and expense by taking on the chewier cases myself. In any event, yesterday evening, two bodies were brought to the morgue, the deaths apparently unrelated, but with one thing in common: both men had evidently taken their own lives." He paused, then added, "One of those men, I'm sorry to say, was Noah Bassett."

"*No.*" Viola sank back in her wheelchair, looking stricken. "Oh, Will, no. Not Noah."

Will glanced at Nell as if for support in being the bearer of such grim tidings. She managed a reassuring look despite her own shock and dismay, having grown quite fond of Mr. Bassett herself from when he and his daughters would visit the house.

"I was dreading giving you this news, but I know how much your friendship with the Bassetts means to you. I'd wanted to tell you myself before you read about it in the morning paper." Uncrossing his legs, Will leaned forward to rest his elbows on his knees.

"Thank you, Will." Viola shook her head listlessly. "I wish I could say it comes as a shock that Noah would . . . do something like that, but given the way his life's gone these past few years . . . Was he ruined in the gold crash, do you know?"

"One can only assume so, but I'll need to find out for sure. To draw a reliable conclusion about a death like this, one must examine not only the victim's body, but his life—his state of mind, his situation, the circumstances in which he died. Which is partly why I'm here, to help fill in those blanks. However, the evidence so far does indicate that Mr. Bassett died by his own hand."

"How . . ." Viola hesitated, as if she wasn't sure she really wanted to know. "How did he . . ."

With a glance at Gracie, Will lowered his voice and said, "He apparently locked himself in his bedroom, filled his bathtub with warm water, and opened both radial arteries with—"

"Radial?"

"He cut his wrists," Nell said as she smoothed out the glue.

"With a pen knife," Will added. "His death resulted from massive blood loss."

Viola closed her eyes, color leaching from her face. "Noah, Noah . . . He was my age exactly, fifty-nine. Our birthdays were only a week apart."

"His daughter found him," Will said.

"Which one?" Nell asked. "He's got two, and they both live with him."

"Her name is Miriam."

"She's the eldest," Viola said. "About your age, I suspect, mid-thirties or so."

"A spinster?" Will asked.

"Not for long. She's engaged to a professor at Harvard Divinity School—Martin's favorite professor, as a matter of fact, the Reverend John Tanner."

"Really?" Nell said. "I always sort of assumed Dr. Tanner was married—but perhaps that's just because he's a clergyman."

"You know him?" Will asked.

Nell nodded. "Martin's had him over to the house a few times. He seems like a pleasant fellow."

"Your father can't bear him, because he's a Unitarian," Viola said, "but I agree with Nell. He seems like a good man, and I think he's the right sort for Miriam. She's the type one would never suspect of having been born into great wealth. She reminded me of Noah in that way—of how he used to be. Mature, pragmatic, capable . . . I'm glad she's the one who found Noah, and not Becky."

"Becky's the younger sister?" Will asked.

"Yes. Rebecca, but everyone calls her Becky. Just turned nineteen, I believe, but she seems younger. One of those chatty, chipper young girls, you know? But quite likable, really."

"There are just the two daughters?" Will asked. "That's quite a gap between children."

"They had a son in between—Tommy. He died in the war. And Lucy, Noah's wife—his late wife—suffered a number of sad events during those years, as well."

"Sad events?" Will asked.

"Miscarriages," Nell said. Viola didn't normally resort to euphemisms, but she was was exceptionally tender-hearted when it came to the subject of children.

"It was heartbreaking," Viola said, "watching her lose all those babies. Lucy Bassett was the warmest, most generous and patient soul I've ever known—the perfect wife for Noah. All she ever wanted was to have a houseful of children to love and take care of. She had no problem having Miriam, but then it took her so long to carry a second child to full term. Miriam was eleven when Tommy was born. There was at least one other disappointment after that. I know Noah wanted her to stop trying for more children, because it was just too upsetting for her, and she wasn't that young anymore, but then Becky came along. 'My little gift from God,' Lucy called her. Unfortunately, her health started deteriorating after that. She died of cancer when Becky was just three years old."

"How did her husband react to her death?" Will asked.

"Oh, he was devastated. It tore him apart. He was a wonderful man, you know, but far too easily bruised for his own good." Viola's voice was hoarser than usual; her eyes shone wetly. She groped under the cuff of her smock for the handkerchief she kept tucked in her dress sleeve.

Will shook his out and handed it to her.

Dabbing her eyes, Viola said, "Poor Noah, he was never the same after that. He was quite a large man, you know—tall and big-boned, and always, well, a bit on the stocky side, with these great, bushy mutton-chop whiskers. I used to think of him as a giant, kindly bear. He was a very popular fellow, the kind of warmhearted man everyone loved. But after he lost Lucy, he became more like a . . . well, one of those big, shambling dogs that always looks a bit sad and confused. Then, when he lost Tommy right before the war ended, he just seemed to . . . gradually collapse. He retreated into himself, neglected his appearance, stopped calling on his friends. We paid a New Year's Day call on him this year, Nell and Gracie and Martin and I. Miriam told us he was still in bed—at one-thirty in the afternoon."

Will said, "I'll need to speak to his daughters before I can confidently label it a suicide, but if he'd been mentally depressed for a number of years, that would make it all the more likely that a major financial loss might send him over the edge. Mr. Munro's case is a bit woollier, I'm afraid."

"*Philip* Munro?" Viola asked.

Will nodded. "He was the other man I autopsied yesterday."

"Oh, my word," Viola said. "He's so young. *Was* so young."

"Thirty-nine," Will said. "You knew him, obviously."

"We all knew him, everyone. Well, everyone in a certain circle." Nell knew she meant the circle of Boston's Brahmin elite. It was a tight-knit, exclusive little cosmos unto itself, governed by a rigid code of conduct. She said, "Your brother Harry knew him particularly well. They'd become bosom friends in the past year or so."

"Really?" Will said. "Munro's more than ten years older than Harry."

"They were both bachelors, though, and of like temperament, and after Harry moved out of the house, they lived only two or three blocks apart in the Back Bay. And if you want to know the truth, I do believe there was a fair amount of hero worship involved. I'm told Harry idolized Mr. Munro."

"Even more than he idolizes himself?" Will said aridly.

Viola said, "Actually, yes. Mr. Munro was older and even richer than Harry, a self-made, charismatic man about town. Handsome, roguish, athletic . . . and something of a rakehell, which must have appealed enormously to Harry." She shook her head. "It's just so hard to believe. Philip Munro, of all people."

"Why does it surprise you so?" Will asked.

"Well, he was . . . *Philip Munro*. He was just so . . . on top of it all, so confident—to the point of arrogance, but one can hardly blame him. He was indecently rich, you know. New money—his father had been a schoolteacher in Brookline—but it was money nonetheless, and in this city, that counts for something."

"So does lineage," Will said. "Was he truly accepted by the old guard? Did they let him into the Somerset Club? Did they whisper behind his back?" It was precisely the question Nell would have asked.

"Well . . ." Viola appeared to ponder the question. "Boston isn't quite as bad as New York, where you've got to be a sixth-generation Knickerbocker before they'll even acknowledge one's existence. Still, there *is* a caste system here, and although they admire achievements, especially as regards business endeavors, I'm afraid it's pedigree that counts in the long run."

It was always *they* when Viola discussed Boston society, not *we*. Having retained many of the *bohème* ideals of her youth, she'd never truly felt at home in her husband's world of wealth and propriety.

"No, they never invited him into the Somerset," Viola continued. "And there were whispers, to be sure, but they weren't so much about his lack of breeding as about, well, the way he conducted his private life—although the one was generally blamed for the other."

"If Munro's private life was anything like Harry's," Will observed, "I don't doubt he raised a few eyebrows. Especially given his age. Thirty-nine might seem young to you, ma'am, but it strikes me as a bit long in the tooth to be larking about with reprobates like Harry on drunken night sprees and the like."

"Philip Munro was a firebrand, there's no denying that," Viola said. "They say he brought that same sense of daring and recklessness to his business transactions, did insanely risky things, yet he always came out on top."

"What sort of business did he engage in?" Will asked.

"I believe it had to do with the stock market, mostly, though I confess I'm at a loss as to exactly what it was he did. Those sorts of things—stocks, commodities—they're utterly foreign to me. Your father disapproved of him, said he wasn't so much a businessman as a gambler. What was it he called him? A *'nouveau riche* raider.' Oh, and he had connections—friends in New York and Washington, important, powerful men, the kind who share information and help one another out. I understand he dined with President Grant, he and some of his financier friends, when the president came to Boston in June for the Peace Jubilee."

"That can't have hurt his business," Will said.

"He made buckets of money, and his money made more money. Before long the men here in Boston who'd once snickered at him were lining up at his door for advice on how to do the same thing—not your father, of course, but most of the others. Munro's *back* door, mind you. No respectable gentleman wanted to be connected too closely to the likes of Philip Munro."

"Mustn't be seen paying a call on the man," Will said, "but they didn't mind handing over their purses?"

Viola smiled. "Yes, but they handed them over empty and got them back full. Mr. Munro wasn't afraid of money, or vaguely ashamed of it, the way the rest of them are. He bought and sold and connived and speculated as if it were all a game and he could invent and reinvent the rules as he went along."

"Did he always win?" Will asked.

"Often enough to keep some of the most powerful men in Boston in his thrall."

"Was he in league with those Goldbugs, do you know?" Will meant Jay Gould and his cronies, whose greedy machinations had forced President Grant to sell off some of the government's supply in order to lower its price, resulting in yesterday's devastating market collapse. Gould was by far the most notorious Wall Street raider alive, and now the most loathed. Anyone who'd owned gold at noon yesterday, when its value plummeted—and that was a great many people—took a cruel beating. Thousands of investors were left in complete financial ruin.

Viola said, "I don't think anyone was ever really privy to what he bought and sold, just that he made mountains of money doing it. If he *was* a gold speculator, let's hope he didn't talk Harry into getting involved in it."

"You didn't mind Harry befriending a blighter like Munro?" Will asked.

"That question," Viola said with a sardonic smile, "implies that I enjoy some measure of influence over what Harry does and with whom. Of course I disapproved of Mr. Munro—not because of his background, needless to say, but because of his behavior. But he's the reason your brother started playing cricket at the Peabody Club up in Cambridge, which I was actually quite pleased about. I thought it might be good for Harry to get a bit of fresh air and exercise. I'm surprised he never asked you to come along."

Choosing his words with obvious care, Will said, "Harry and I don't see very much of each other."

Not, Nell reflected, since the thorough beating Will dealt his brother last year after learning of Harry's

absinthe-fueled attempt to force himself on Nell—
something Viola would never, God willing, find out about.

"Harry will take this *very* hard," Viola murmured, staring out the window at her little English-style garden, all
tangled and leggy, the way it got every year at the end of
the summer, no matter how hard Viola worked on it.
"How did he die?" she asked without turning from the
window.

"That's debatable, as far as I'm concerned. He was
found on the front steps of his house on Marlborough Street,
beneath the open window of his office on the fourth floor.
It seems fairly clear that he fell that distance, but there are
no witnesses. He's got an unwed sister who lives with him,
but I'm told she was napping when it happened, and none
of the servants actually saw him fall. He was pretty badly
smashed up, but in a way that makes me doubt that he died
from the fall itself."

"I wan out of chalk." Gracie was standing over her artwork, a stub of chalk in her hand, squirming in a way that
instantly put Nell on the alert. "Can I have some more?"

Viola, who was within grabbing distance of Gracie,
pulled her close and whispered something in her ear.

"No," the child insisted with an adamant shake of her
head. "I don't need to."

"I think you do."

Crossing one leg over the other, Gracie said, "I just need
another piece of chalk so I can finish."

"First the W.C.," Nell said. "Then I'll fetch you some
more chalk."

"I'll take her," said Viola, gesturing for the child to follow her as she crossed the room, wheels rattling over the

slate. "You'd best finish sizing that canvas before the glue dries up. Come along, Gracie."

Gracie shook her head. "But I don't—"

"We'll stop at the kitchen afterward and have Mrs. Waters make you a nice cup of hot cocoa."

Gracie dropped the chalk and hurried after her nana. "Can I wide on your lap?" she asked as she followed Viola into the hall. "Can I? Please?"

"*Can* you?" Viola challenged.

"*May* I?" she implored, while dancing that little telltale dance. "Please, Nana?"

"Er . . . perhaps on the way back."

Chapter 2

W ILL smiled as he watched them retreat down the hall. Nell saw amusement in his eyes, and pride, and a hint of wonderment at the child he'd created quite by chance one lonely night with a pretty young chambermaid during his last visit to his family.

It had been a Christmas furlough from his service as a Union Army battle surgeon in December of 1863, shortly before he was captured and imprisoned at Andersonville, along with his brother Robbie. After the hellish prison camp claimed Robbie's life, Will escaped and, wounded inside and out, allowed his family to think he was dead for years while he lost himself in a numbing haze of opium smoke and cards.

"What the devil is that stuff, anyway?" Will asked as Nell dipped up another spatula full of warm, gelatinous glue.

"Rabbit skin glue. Canvases have to be sized with this and then primed with gesso before one can paint on them."

"My mother makes you prepare her canvases? And on a Saturday? I thought you had Saturdays off."

"I do," Nell said as she smeared and scraped. "This is *my* canvas, for a painting I'm planning of Martin and some of his divinity school friends rowing on the Charles River. They're going to pose for me next week."

"Which ones are yours?" he asked, scanning the solarium-turned-studio. The only painting he'd ever seen of hers was the portrait of Gracie that she gave him for his birthday in July, which hung over the fireplace in the little library of his Acorn Street house. It captured Gracie's winsome charm, which was why she'd wanted Will to have it, but it was sketchier than her usual work, because she'd been trying to suggest movement as the child played with her dolls.

Nell guided him around the room, pointing out paintings on easels, leaning against walls, and stored in drying racks—portraits and street scenes, mostly, a few interiors.

"Nell, I'm . . . awestruck," he said after he'd viewed them all. "Your handling of light is incredible. These paintings—they glow from within. Why have you never shown me these before?"

"You've never been to the house before, not since I've lived here." Nell turned back to the canvas she was sizing as her face suffused with heat.

"Are you blushing?" There was amusement in his voice as he came up behind her. He liked to make her redden, then tease her about it, and it wasn't hard, with her coloring. Although she wasn't quite a redhead, her hair being a sort of rust-stained brown, she was cursed with the volatile complexion of that breed—pale, translucent skin that sizzled at the drop of an innuendo.

"You are, aren't you?" he asked.

"No." There was something about blushing with pride from Will's praise that made her feel particularly exposed, as if that which lay in the deepest recesses of her heart were emblazoned in scarlet all over her face for the entire world to see.

"I think you are." He was standing so close that his legs rustled the silk faille skirt beneath her smock frock. "What are you . . ."

Her scalp tickled as he slid one of the filbert brushes out of the twist of hair at her nape, loosening it. "Ah, the ever-practical Miseeney," he chuckled.

"You're making it come undone," Nell said over her shoulder, the movement causing the chignon to unfurl heavily down her back. She bent to retrieve the second brush as it clattered onto the slate.

"I've got it," Will said as he stooped to pick it up, bracing a hand on his bad leg.

Nell turned, reaching for the brushes.

"Allow me." Slipping the brushes into his coat pocket, he shook out the rope of hair and slowly combed his fingers through it, sending little shivers of pleasure into her scalp.

"You know how to put a lady's hair up?" she asked, heavy-lidded from the gentle pulling and tugging.

"I know quite a few things I probably shouldn't." Will gathered up her hair, his long fingers grazing the back of her neck, and twisted the thick, wavy hank into a knot. She wished it didn't feel as good as it did, because she wanted it to go on and on, whereas she probably shouldn't even be letting him do it. It was a rather intimate thing for a gentleman to do for a lady, the sort of thing one might do for a wife. Or a mistress.

Of course, a liaison of that nature was unthinkable in Nell's present circumstances, and not just because she still had a husband in Charleston State Prison—a fact known only to Will and her current confessor, Father Gorman at St. Stephen's. Viola had made it clear five years ago, when she asked the presumably unwed "Miss Sweeney" to serve as governess, that she expected Nell not only to conduct herself with the utmost propriety, but to forswear marriage while Gracie was young, in order to devote her full attention to her charge. She no doubt still expected it, notwithstanding Nell's friendship with Will, which the rest of Boston society took to be an unofficial betrothal—an assumption Will encouraged, since it permitted him to spend time with Nell and his daughter without raising eyebrows. Only Viola and August—and of course, Father Gorman—knew that the courtship was just a façade. They were also the only people in Boston, aside from Nell and Will, who knew that Viola Hewitt's adopted daughter had actually been sired by her son.

"Tell me if this is too tight," Will said as he slid one of the brushes into the twist of hair he'd made, pushing it through the thick knot and out the other side. He did the same with the second brush. *"Eh voilà,"* he murmured, letting his hands linger on her shoulders for a moment before removing them.

Nell patted the chignon, impressed with how solidly it held. "I couldn't have done better myself."

"Surgeon's hands," he said.

That comment reminded her of the autopsies he'd performed yesterday evening. She shook her head as she dipped up some more rabbit glue. "How awful about Mr. Bassett. I feel so sorry for his daughters. They were always so kind and gracious to me. Some of your mother's callers treat me like one of the scullery maids."

"That's because you have an Irish name," Will said, "not because you're a governess. Since a governess is usually just a well-born lady in reduced circumstances, they're considered social equals more or less. An Irishwoman, on the other hand, is, well, *Irish*. I've traveled all over the world, and I think it's fair to say the Irish are more loathed in Boston than anywhere I've been—more so than New York, or even London. But Bassett's daughters like you, eh?"

"They seem to." She skimmed the last of the glue off and turned to look at him. "Why?"

"I'm going to be paying a call on them later, and I'm thinking it might help if you came along. You could introduce me, assure them I'm an all right sort, encourage them to answer my questions."

"An Irish governess vouching for a Hewitt?" Nell said as she wiped off her spatula, having sealed the entire canvas.

"Most of my parents' circle, except for old family friends like the Pratts and the Thorpes, have never met me. Some of them don't even know I exist. Somehow I doubt Saint August would bring me up in casual conversation. If he does, God knows what he says. You, on the other hand, are a familiar presence to anyone who's spent any time with my mother these past few years. And of course, you're now presumed to be her prospective daughter-in-law. You'll be trading in that troublesome Irish surname for one of the oldest and most respected names in Boston."

"Presumably."

"Presumably."

"How long do you suppose we can keep up this sham courtship?" she asked.

"Long engagements are *de rigueur* in Boston society. We could go on this way for years without causing comment."

Nell set a battered, enameled bowl on her worktable. "I'll go with you to the Bassetts. You're right—what with everything they're going through right now, it'll be best if I'm there to reassure them."

"I appreciate that. Anything I can do to help?" he asked as she opened the little storage cabinet in which she kept her supplies.

"Thanks, but I'm just mixing up a batch of gesso to prime the canvas with. It's a one-person job." Fetching down a jar of white pigment, she said, "You might want to keep your distance until I get this stuff bound. It's powdered lead."

Backing away, he said, "You do take measures to keep from breathing that in, don't you?"

Nell pulled a kerchief from the pocket of her smock. "This from the gentleman who persists in inhaling tobacco smoke despite all the warnings from, let's see . . . the medical journals, *Harper's Weekly,* your good friend Isaac Foster, who happens to be a pulmonary expert . . ."

"I've cut down substantially just to get you and Foster off my back. I only light up nowadays as a sort of . . . inhalable nerve tonic, something to soothe me and keep me occupied when I can't quite abide the world and my role in it."

"Does that happen very often?" Nell asked.

"Much less than it did before I . . ." *Before I met you?* "Before I returned to Boston. My point is, if I quit altogether, I'll have no bad habits left at all, and that's far too dreary a prospect to contemplate."

Tying the kerchief around her nose and mouth, Nell unscrewed the jar, carefully filled an eight-ounce scoop, and tipped it into the bowl. She dribbled in enough glue to work the powder into a harmless paste, then pushed down her makeshift mask.

"Actually, there *is* something you can do for me." Pointing to the big sack of whiting under the table, she said, "Would you mind pulling that out?"

Will crouched down to retrieve the sack. "What's in here?" he asked, grunting with effort as he dragged it out.

"White marble dust. Chalk or gypsum would do, but your mother likes marble."

"Only the best for Lady Viola, eh?"

Untying the sack, Nell scooped up eight ounces of the talcum-fine powder and added it to the lead paste. "I must say, Will, it's gratifying to see you take such an interest in your work for Harvard, especially given the arm-twisting Isaac had to go through to get you on board."

"He's probably regretting it right now."

"Nonsense." Nell poured a scoop of warm glue into the bowl and mixed it with a wooden spoon. "I've seen Isaac and Emily two or three times since the fall term started, and he assures me you're a brilliant teacher."

"It's the research side of things where I'm developing a bit of a reputation. My colleagues regard me, some of them anyway, as a foreign-educated dilettante who got where he is through nepotism—which is entirely true, of course. They know I specialized in forensics at Edinburgh, but they're not at all convinced it's a valid field of study. My methods and the conclusions I draw are greeted with no end of hilarity by a number of my peers, and the Philip Munro case is no exception. Isaac had a couple of the anatomy professors review my autopsy findings yesterday— standard procedure—and they agreed I'm utterly daft for thinking it might be anything other than a suicide."

"If they knew you as I do," she said with a smile, "they'd realize you're utterly daft for entirely different reasons."

He leaned against the table, contemplating her. "I've missed our afternoons in the park," he said, his voice soft.

Nell returned her attention to her bowlful of gesso, stirring industriously to rid it of lumps. "Isaac tells me you're held in high regard by the new dean of the medical school. Dr. Ellis, is it?"

Will nodded. "Calvin Ellis—good man. Gratifying though I find his praise, it only serves to further disaffect certain other member of the faculty."

"They're jealous because the dean admires you? One would assume men of that stature would be immune to such a base sentiment."

Chuckling, Will said, "You're still prone to those galloping assumptions, I see. The possession of a medical degree is no guarantee of emotional maturity. I wouldn't care, except that there seems to be a campaign afoot to discredit me in Dr. Ellis's eyes. I have my allies—Foster and a few of the other professors—but it's been my experience that it doesn't take much for people to make trouble for you, if they're bound and determined to do so."

"Why should you care about what they think of you at Harvard?" Nell asked, smiling to herself as she continued to mix the gesso. "After all, you're only there for one term, as a lark."

"I've asked myself that," Will said. "I suppose what it boils down to is that no man likes to look the fool in any endeavor, even one that's of relatively little consequence to him."

Nell looked up from the bowl to gauge Will's sincerity. Was he really so blasé about his professional reputation, or did he care more than he was willing to let on?

Wresting his gaze from hers, he said, "I went to see your detective friend at City Hall yesterday evening."

"Colin Cook?"

Will nodded. "I'd wanted to see if he'd be willing to look into this Philip Munro business, but he said he couldn't touch it—the matter had already been assigned to another detective. Guess which one?"

"Not that ghastly little weasel with the plaid waistcoats and the sneer."

Will nodded grimly. "Charlie Skinner—although I daresay 'ghastly weasel' suits him better. He was still there, so I went in to have a word with him. I shouldn't dream of repeating his, er, greeting, such as it was, in the presence of a lady. Suffice it to say there is no chance he would have helped me even if he didn't loathe me—which he does, to a rather comical degree. He's convinced Munro threw himself out of that window. Won't even offer a reward for information."

"So, if Mr. Munro's death is to be explained as something other than suicide, thereby salvaging your professional reputation, it's up to you to—"

"Thereby not just salvaging my reputation," Will corrected, "but seeing justice done. Even to a selfish lout such as I, the notion of someone bludgeoning a man in the head, then tossing him out the window and walking free . . ." He shook his head.

"What makes you so sure it happened that way?" Nell asked as she worked the last few lumps out of the gesso. "Someone who's fallen four stories onto a flight of stone entrance steps must end up pretty, well . . ."

"Oh, he was a mess, all right, but as far as I can tell, the wounds to his trunk and limbs appeared to have been acquired postmortem. There's a difference in appearance, you know, between injuries sustained during life and those done to a body after death. The bones of a dead man are difficult to break, and they break differently than those of someone who's alive. Take the ribs. In a living man, they'll splinter apart. In someone who's already dead, if they break at all, they'll more or less crack neatly."

"And Mr. Munro's ribs?" Nell paused in her stirring to shake out her aching arm; those lumps were stubborn.

"Completely intact but for a couple of hairline cracks. Here, give me that," Will said as he lifted the spoon from her hand and took over the stirring. "Also, with the vast majority of his wounds, there was no sign of any vital reaction. No inflammation, no hemorrhage, no suppuration . . . He was bashed up, yes, but in the way a cadaver might be bashed up if it was dropped four tall stories."

"With the exception of his head?" Nell surmised, given what he'd said about the bludgeoning.

"He had several compound depressed fractures of the skull, as if a blunt, elongated object had been applied to a small area with extreme force. Most of these were basal and occipital fractures. Unlike his other injuries, these head wounds were almost certainly sustained while he was still living. Cranial bones, especially those at the base of the skull, are nearly impossible to break postmortem."

"Hence your theory that he was hit over the head and tossed out the window," Nell said.

"That's how I see it, but my critics at Harvard think it's all humbug. They think his head struck the cornice over the front porch on the way down—which was presumably what killed him, since it's actually possible to survive a fall of that height, even onto hard stone steps. But an injury like that would produce a skull fracture that's linear, not depressed, and there would be much less extravasation of blood within the cranial cavity. I wouldn't mind having a look at that cornice, though, just to see what we're dealing with." He handed Nell the bowlful of creamy, lump-free gesso. "Do you have to apply this now, or—"

"No, it can wait," she said as she covered it with a rag. "What about the front of his head? His face?"

"Smashed, as one would expect. Few vital reactions in that area."

"But some?"

Will shrugged. "The nose could have been broken before death. It's hard to tell when there's so much—"

"Uncle Will!" Gracie called out as she darted into the room. "Nana says I can invite you to my birthday tea!"

"She did?"

"It's tomowwow afternoon," Gracie said, bobbing up and down the way she did when she was excited. "And there's going to be cake, and all my fwiends will be there, and Mr. Thurston and Miseeney. Please say you'll come. Please?"

"Mr. Thurston" was Maxmillian Thurston, the celebrated playwright, who'd forged a close friendship of late with Nell and Will. Flamboyant, witty, and warm-natured, he'd become a sort of surrogate grandfather to Gracie.

Viola, wheeling into the room, said, "Do come to the tea, Will, if only for a little while. It would mean so much to us, and well, I'm quite sure your father shan't be there."

"A birthday tea, eh?" Crouching down, Will gathered his daughter in his arms. "I wouldn't miss it for the world."

Chapter 3

"**E**ILEEN!" called a girlish voice from inside the house after Will tapped the door knocker for the second time. It was a brass lion's head knocker, filmed with tarnish.

The Bassett home, one of the few freestanding townhouses on Beacon Hill, was an imposing redbrick edifice that had probably been built around the end of the last century. The house looked weathered, and not charmingly so. The black-painted door and shutters needed scraping, the mortar repointing, the lawns watering. So choked with weeds and moss was the driveway that one could hardly see the cobblestones.

"Eileen, the door!"

About half a minute passed before the door finally swung open, courtesy of a shapely strawberry blonde dressed entirely in black: Becky Bassett. She smiled when she recognized Nell. "Miss Sweeney." She glanced up at Will, as if trying to place him, then back at Nell. "The girl should have answered the door. I don't know where she is."

Becky had one of those voices that had stopped maturing at around the age of eight; no matter how old she got, she would always sound like a little child. The effect was reinforced by her soft features and big, guileless blue eyes.

Nell said, "I'm so sorry to disturb you at a time like this. Miss Bassett, allow me to introduce Dr. William Hewitt."

Will doffed his hat and bowed. "My condolences, Miss Bassett."

"Thank you." Becky stuck a needle and thread into the square of white fabric in her hand, which Nell had at first taken for a handkerchief. On closer inspection, it appeared to be a half-sewn cuff of white muslin, most likely intended for the dress Becky had on—a mourning gown with a drop-shouldered yoke and elaborate piping, generously trimmed in black silk crepe. It was a lovely dress, or would have been had it not pulled slightly across a too snugly corseted bosom, as if it were a size too small.

From somewhere in the house came a pungent, vinegary aroma.

"Is your sister at home?" Nell asked.

"Yes, of course. Miriam's been in and out of the kitchen all morning." Becky gestured them into a front hall that struck Nell, despite its lofty ceiling and palatial staircase, as timeworn and cheerless. The hallstand was water stained, the walls decorated with a hodgepodge of cheap and mundane steel engravings. Imprinted here and there on the wallpaper, an outmoded design of classical urns and swags, were ghostly shadows of the paintings that had once graced these walls. The staircase rose to a landing lit by a tall, arched window that would have looked quite striking had it not been marred by two cracked panes.

Leading them toward the back of the house, Becky said, "My sister always needs to be doing things. If there's no work to be done, she'll invent some, especially when she's fretting about something, and she's always fretting about something. Of course, with what happened to Papa, one can understand, I suppose, but even when everything's going along splendidly, she always has to be tending to things and making sure everything's just so . . ."

She guided them around the staircase to the left, through an anteroom that housed the service stairwell, past a china room with nearly bare shelves, and into the sweltering kitchen, babbling on all the while. "Dash it," Becky said. "She was here just a few minutes ago."

The kitchen was enormous but gloomy. Occupying most of the back wall was a fireplace in which a copper wash boiler simmered away over low flames, a three-pronged dolly stick balanced across its top. On the hearth sat a ceramic jar labeled *Blue Vitriol* and a burlap sack half-filled with small, dark wood chips. Nell scooped up a handful and sniffed them: logwood, not an unpleasant scent, but one she would forever associate with death. "Your sister is dyeing clothes?" She peered into the inky liquid seething in the pot.

Becky smiled indulgently, as if Miriam's industriousness were a character flaw one must put up with. "Like I said, she's always got to be doing something. We've both got mourning dresses left over from when poor Tommy passed, but she says they don't fit her like they used to. Well, neither do mine, but I'd rather wear something nice than some outmoded old frock I've gone and dyed. They never look right, you know, and they run in the rain, and the dye rubs off no matter how careful you are . . ."

Becky Bassett was one of those females—they're mostly females—who can maintain an interminable stream of patter without the apparent need to inhale. "Bad enough to have to wear black for a whole year," she continued with a delicate little shudder. "I look sickly in black, positively consumptive. But to wear something that's black *and* shabby . . . it's simply too much. And I've seen those dresses when they try to bleach them back. They're never the same as before, always a bit washed out and . . ." She looked toward the front of the house as a knock came at the door. "More visitors?"

"People will have read about what happened in the paper," Nell said. "They'll be wanting to make condolence calls. You go ahead and answer the door. Dr. Hewitt and I can wait."

As Becky retreated back up the hall, Nell lifted the dolly stick, dipped it two-handed into the copper boiler, and hauled up a mass of sodden silk—the ruffled skirt of a dress. It evidently hadn't been steeping very long, having absorbed only enough of the black dye to impart a grayish cast to the original yellow and pink stripes.

"Miriam is ruining this pretty dress for nothing," Nell said. "Vivid patterns are hard to cover up. She'll never get it entirely black."

"An expert on dyeing clothes now, are you?" Will asked with a smile.

She didn't answer, merely shoved the silk back into the pot and gave it a stir, for all the good it would do. From the corner of her eye, she saw Will's smile fade as he deciphered her silence: Someone who'd seen her family succumb one by one to the wretched diseases bred by poverty would have learned a thing or two about making clothes black.

He rubbed his neck, let out a hefty sigh. "You should tell me when I'm being thick, Nell. I'd hate for you to think ill of me just because I can't hear what's coming out of my own mouth."

"I could never think ill of you," she said, poking at the contents of the copper simply to avoid having to look at him.

"You did when you first met me."

"You were a different man then. You didn't care about anything or anyone, even yourself."

"Opium is a demanding mistress," Will said. "The men she enslaves worship her and her alone—but in return, she purges one's universe of pain."

"And of every other human feeling," Nell said as she turned to face him.

"An unholy covenant, to be sure, but it served me well enough." He smiled in that serenely intimate way of his. "Until I was wrested from the arms of Morphia by a certain willful young Irish governess."

"You freed *yourself* from that poison," she said. "I had nothing to do with it."

He looked at her, his head tilted slightly, almost smiling, but in an odd, grave way that telegraphed his response well enough: *You think not?*

She looked away from him, unsettled more by the things that went unspoken between them than by the things they said aloud. Her gaze fell on the hearth rug, which was stained with splashes of dye. Droplets trailed off onto the worn plank floor, ending at a door to the right of the fireplace—the back door of the house.

Will, having noticed the same thing, opened the door and gestured Nell outside. They followed the trail of dye along a flagstone garden path that detoured around the right side of the carriage house. Leaning drunkenly against it was a dilapidated wooden hut with a tin roof, its door standing open. A willow basket sat on the hard-packed dirt, empty but for a pair of damp black stockings at the very bottom.

"Miss Bassett?" Nell said.

Miriam Bassett appeared in the doorway of the drying shed, her pale blond hair wrapped in a kerchief, a dye-spattered apron tied over her brown dress. She was as generous in shape as her younger sister, but taller, and with the sturdy, robust look of someone who kept herself active. With both hands she held a dripping black garment that reeked of wet wool and logwood dye. Anyone meeting her for the first time would take her for a maidservant.

"Miss Sweeney," Miriam said, seeming a bit dazed, or

maybe just tired. Nell had always thought of her as having a distinctive, sharply carved kind of beauty, but this morning, with her puffy eyes, and ruddy nose, she looked haggard. Looking at Will and then down at herself, she said, "I'm sorry I'm not ready to receive callers yet. I ought to be. The morning has gotten away from me."

"*I'm* sorry for intruding," Nell said. "Please accept my apologies, and my deepest sympathy. I was very fond of your father."

Miriam nodded abjectly and looked down, wringing the garment onto the dirt with dark-stained hands. The interior of the shed was murky, but Nell could make out the freshly dyed items Miriam had just hung up to dry on a wooden clothes crane: a flounced linen petticoat, corset cover, and corset.

Nell was about to introduce Will when a man's voice called from the direction of the house, "Miss Bassett?"

Miriam, suddenly animated, said, "Over here," as she stepped out onto the flagstone walk.

The gentleman striding toward them—Reverend John Tanner—was as tall as Will, and not much older, but his spectacles and prematurely silver-threaded hair suggested the kind of dignity one normally associated with advanced years. He was a handsome man in a certain rangy, scholastic way. Like Will, he was clean-shaven, with short-trimmed sideburns, imparting, correctly or not, the aura of the aesthete. His attire—a black frock coat that floated around his lanky frame, black trousers, black vest, black tie, black gloves—was appropriately, if unintentionally, funereal; Nell had never seen him dressed any other way.

The minister came up to Miriam as if Nell and Will weren't even there, both hands clutching his hat, an old-fashioned, Quakerish wideawake. "I just found out. Are you all right?"

She closed her eyes, nodding. "Thank you, Dr. Tanner. Yes, I'm . . . managing."

He frowned at her, squinted into the drying shed. "What in blazes are you doing? Can't Eileen do this?"

Miriam unwound the twist of fabric in her hands, which turned out to be a large, fringed shawl. "I sent her upstairs." She shook out the shawl. "To clean Papa's bedroom."

Tanner regarded her in obvious bafflement.

Nell said, "It was in his bedroom that . . . it happened."

Tanner closed his eyes on a sigh. "That, er, that wasn't in the paper, just that he . . ." The minister shook his head. "None of the details."

Miriam cleared her throat. "Miss Nell Sweeney . . ." She gestured from Nell to Tanner. "My fiancé, the Reverend Dr. Jonathan Tanner."

"Miss Sweeney and I have met," Tanner said with a bow. "You're Mrs. August Hewitt's companion, are you not?"

"The governess, officially," Nell said. "It's good to see you again, Reverend—although I wish the circumstances were different. Miss Bassett, Dr. Tanner, may I introduce Dr. William Hewitt."

Will bowed to Miriam and shook Tanner's hand.

"Dr. Hewitt is Martin's eldest brother," Nell told them. "He's also the surgeon who performed the postmortem on your father, Miss Bassett."

"The purpose of the examination," Will explained, "was to establish the cause of death. But I'm afraid I can't finalize my conclusion until I investigate not just his body, but the circumstances surrounding his demise."

"There's nothing much to investigate." Miriam gave the shawl a final spattering shake, turned, and carried it back into the drying shed. "I came home and found him on the floor of his room, next to the bathtub he kept under his bed. He'd cut his wrists."

Dr. Tanner pushed his spectacles up his acquiline nose, whispering something under his breath that didn't sound very ministerial. He ducked into the shed, hovering over his fiancée as she spread the big square of damp black wool on a wooden rack. "Blast it all," he said, "I hate to see you slaving away at a time like this. You should be having this conversation inside, in the front parlor, where it's cool and quiet. I'll make you a pot of tea."

"I'd rather keep busy."

"Miss Bassett." Tanner's voice was gentle, but tinged ever so slightly with exasperation. "Please."

She straightened up, rubbing the small of her back. "Could you do something for me, Dr. Tanner? Papa needs . . ." looking down, she said, "He needs a suit of clothes to be laid out in, and I . . . I can't bear to set foot in that room, much less go in there and start sorting through his things."

"Of course." He rested a hand on her arm, just for a moment; Nell wouldn't have been surprised if this was the first time he'd ever touched her. Quietly he said, "But you must promise me that you'll stop all this. Come inside. I'll wager you haven't even had breakfast yet."

"There's a dress in the dye pot," she said. "I just need to get that hung up and then empty out the pot and clean things up in the kitchen. If you'll just go up to Papa's room and pick out some clothes . . . His best frock coat, you'll know it when you see it, and his gray trousers—the good ones, not the mended ones—and—"

"I'll see to it." Tanner patted her arm. "Don't give it another thought."

"While you're up there . . ." Miriam glanced through the doorway at Nell and Will, then turned away to smooth out the already smooth shawl. What she said then was spoken so softly that even her fiancé, standing right next to her, had to bend his head to hear her better.

"Papers?" he asked. "You mean—"

Miriam closed a hand around his arm and said something else. Will cast an inquiring glance at Nell, who was standing closer to the shed than he. She made a show of peering at her pendant watch while angling an ear toward the doorway, but she couldn't make out Miriam's words, just her tone of restrained distress.

"I'll take a look." Tanner was the kind of man whose whisper could be heard half a block away. As he backed out of the shed, he exhorted Miriam again to abandon her labors and go inside, then nodded to Nell and Will and returned to the house.

Miriam came out of the shed and bent to retrieve a stocking from the basket. It was an indication of her distracted state of mind that she didn't seem to care whether a strange gentleman saw her underpinnings.

"So you came home and found your father in his room," Will said. "What time would you say that was?"

Miriam shrugged. "Late afternoon. Four, four-fifteen."

"Where had you been?"

Frowning, she balled up the stocking to squeeze it out. "Running errands. You can't honestly have any doubt as to how he died, Dr. Hewitt."

"I believe he died by his own hand," Will said. "But before I can officially attest to it, I need a little more information. Did you go directly to your father's room when you came home?"

Miriam pulled out a clothespin, which she studied pensively. "I, um, yes, I believe so."

"Why?" Will asked.

With a twitch of her shoulders, she said, "If one wanted to see him, that was where one went. He spent his days there, for the most part." Turning, Miriam retreated back into the drying shed to hang up the stocking. Raising her voice a bit to be heard, she said, "It's two connected rooms—bedroom in front, study in back."

"Is that where he saw to his business matters?" Will asked.

A pause. "At one time."

"And lately?"

The pause was longer this time. Miriam emerged from the shed looking grim. "My father hasn't been himself— *hadn't* been himself—since my mother passed away back in 'fifty-three. Then, four years ago, he lost my brother, his only son, just as the war was ending. I've never been privy to his business transactions, but one can only assume he'd neglected them for some time, given . . . well, our declining circumstances. He slept a great deal. Took a little too much wine at dinner, a little too much port before bed. He craved oblivion, Dr. Hewitt, and one afternoon he clearly decided to make it permanent. That's all I can tell you. It's all I know."

Snatching up the second stocking, she squeezed it out and took it into the shed.

Nell said, "Do you know if he had invested in gold?"

Miriam draped the stocking over an arm of the crane, tugging and pulling to reshape it, her back to them. "Papa never talked about such matters with the family—nothing having to do with money, ever. He considered it unseemly."

"Then you wouldn't know whether his suicide had anything to do with the collapse of the gold market yesterday?" Will asked.

"I told you, he'd been melancholic for years. Perhaps the general atmosphere of despair yesterday sent him over the edge—so many men losing everything."

"He knew about the gold crash, then?" Nell asked. "Despite his being holed up in his room most of the time?"

There came a long pause, then Miriam sighed heavily. "The *Boston Daily Advertiser* printed an extra early in the afternoon, and I took it up to him before I left for my errands. He knew what was happening."

"You never did tell us why you went to his room later yesterday afternoon, after your errands," Will said. "You said you knew you'd find him there, but not why you wanted to see him."

A moment passed, and then she came out of the shed, wiping her hands on her apron. "I'd gotten into the habit of checking up on him, trying to wake him up if he was napping, seeing if there was anything he needed . . ."

"I understand his bedroom door was locked," Will said.

"Yes."

"That was unusual?"

"It was. It worried me, especially after I knocked and called to him, and got no answer."

"What did you do?"

"I called down to Eileen to fetch the key from the butler's pantry."

"Eileen is a maid?" he asked.

"*The* maid. We've had to let the others go."

"What did you find when you opened the door?"

Miriam looked off toward the house, the morning sunlight shimmering in her eyes.

"Will," Nell said quietly, "perhaps we can continue this some other—"

"He was lying on his stomach with his hands in the bathtub," she said in a damp, strained voice. "It's one of those shallow tin tubs with a wide lip to keep the water from splashing onto the floor—you know the kind. He had his coat off and his sleeves rolled up. His face was resting on the lip—the flat, seat part of it—as if it were a pillow, and his arms . . ." She illustrated his position by turning her head to the side and raising her bent arms over her head.

"The knife he used," Will said. "Was it there?"

Miriam nodded. "It was the pen knife from his desk. It was on the rug next to him. There was b-blood everywhere—the floor, the w-wall—" She hitched in a breath and closed her eyes.

Will reached into his pocket for his handkerchief, but he'd given it to his mother earlier. Nell pulled hers out of the chatelaine on her belt and offered it to Miriam, but she waved it away. Drawing in a tremulous breath, she said, "I'm—I'm all right. I just . . . I can't afford to fall apart today. There's too much to do."

"I'd like to see your father's bedroom, if I may," Will said.

"Why? I . . . I've told you everything. I've described it all for you."

"Yes, but if I could see it for myself, it would help me to—"

"I'm sorry," Miriam said. "I've answered your questions, I've told you everything you wanted to know. That room, it's . . ." She shook her head. "I can't even bear to think about it. It . . . it was the last place my father was alive, the place where he took his life. *I* haven't even been in there. The thought of strangers trooping through it . . ."

"*You* haven't been in there?" Nell asked. "But you were the one who . . . found him."

"I went no farther than the doorway," she said. "I was . . . horrified. Grief-stricken. My throat was sore afterward from screaming. But I never stepped into that room. Eileen did, to make sure he was really dead, but I . . . I couldn't. I still can't."

"I'll be with Dr. Hewitt when he's in there," Nell said. "We'll respect the room. We shan't touch anything."

"I'm sorry," Miriam repeated. "I just can't have it. And it should hardly be necessary. I've told you what happened."

Will looked as if he wanted to press the point, but after considering it a moment, he merely said, "Just one more question if I may, Miss Bassett, and then we'll leave you in peace."

"There was no note," Miriam said as she lifted the empty basket.

Will looked at her.

"Isn't that what you wanted to know?" Miriam asked.

"As a matter of fact, it is. Did you *look* for a note?"

"Yes."

"But if you didn't even enter the room—" Nell began.

"Eileen looked. I asked her to. There was no note." Miriam tucked the basket snugly up against her hip. "Now, if you'll excuse me, I have things I need to do. I'll have Becky show you out."

B ECKY prattled on about her father's final arrangements as she held the front door open for Nell and Will.

"Miriam wants to have the funeral Tuesday afternoon. She wants Dr. Tanner to give the eulogy, and of course he's the perfect gentleman to do it, being a man of the cloth and such a splendid speaker, not to mention having known Papa so well. I wish he could perform the funeral service itself, but Miriam says that would be wrong, because of course, he's a Unitarian, and Papa was a Congregationalist, never mind that he hadn't been to church in years." She winced. "Which I'm not supposed to mention, so please forget I said it. Anyway, the service will be at Central Congregational on Newbury, even though Reverend Bingham there has never even met Papa, which seems rather sad to me, but Miriam says that's the way Papa would have wanted it, and she should know, because she was really much closer to him than I was, so it seems only right that she should have the final say in the arrangements. Not that

Papa and I were on bad terms, or anything like that, it's just that he never sat and talked to me the way he talked to Miriam, so—"

"So I don't suppose you'd know anything about your father's business dealings," Nell interjected. "Whether he'd invested in gold?"

"Oh goodness, no, he never discussed such things. Mr. Munro was the only person Papa ever talked to about—" Becky cut herself off with a groan. "There I go again. Miriam's right, I'm such a rattle-pate. Please, please, *please* don't tell her I said anything."

Will and Nell exchanged a look. "About Philip Munro?" Nell asked. "Why aren't you supposed to talk about him?"

Becky glanced toward the back of the house and lowered her voice to a whisper. "Miriam doesn't want anyone to know that he had anything to do with us, even now that he's dead. You won't tell her I said anything, will you?"

"Of course not." Nell smiled conspiratorially. "If you don't tell her that Dr. Hewitt and I slipped upstairs for a couple of minutes before we left."

Becky stared at her. Will turned and smiled at Nell in a way that she found very gratifying.

"You want to go upstairs?" Becky asked them.

Will said, "I just want to take a look at your father's room, since it's where he . . . well, to help substantiate the diagnosis of suicide. Your sister was reluctant to let me up there, but you seem a bit less . . . wrought up about things."

A classic Will Hewitt understatement, Nell thought.

From the rear of the house came the creak of the back door opening, and Miriam's footsteps retreating down the flagstone path toward the drying shed.

Becky cocked her head to listen. "She's hanging up that dress, and then she'll have to clean up in the kitchen. It'll take her a little while—twenty minutes, maybe." Shooing them toward the stairs, she said, "If she catches you up there, I had nothing to do with it."

Chapter 4

"MOTHER of God," Nell murmured as they stood in the doorway of Noah Bassett's bedroom.

The maid Eileen was on her hands and knees with her back to them, scrubbing a sudsy bristle brush over the carpet. Being of petite stature, she really had to put her back into it; a little grunt of effort escaped her with every stroke of the brush. Nell closed her eyes, but a ghastly tableau was emblazoned on her mind's eye.

The carpet, an elegant if worn Savonnerie patterned in shades of gold and cream, was smeared with blood, some of which had spurted from Mr. Bassett's slashed arteries onto the counterpane on the half-tester bed. Part of the carpet had already been scrubbed; it was damp and strewn with pink-stained washrags, on one of which lay an ivory-handled pen knife. Two buckets of reddish water, one soapy and one less so, stood next to a bathing pan of tinned sheet iron that resembled an upended garden hat with a wide, curved brim. Blood, or bloody water, filled the tub's shallow well.

Nell took a deep breath, but the stench of old blood mingled with ox-gall soap made the gorge rise in her throat.

Will closed a strong hand around her arm, said her name softly.

She opened her eyes and crossed herself.

Eileen, who'd paused in her scrubbing to survey them over her shoulder, noticed the gesture and cast a curious glance at Nell's blue silk dress and chic little velvet tam. Unlike the young maid, with her sweetly Gaelic visage, one wouldn't necessarily peg Nell as Irish Catholic just by looking at her. More often than not, given her attire and comportment, she was taken for a Brahmin miss of the prim and starchy variety.

Eileen looked from Nell to Will, who was sweeping his gaze around the room, those dark, trenchant eyes seeming to catalog every detail of the scene. To Nell, it looked as if Mr. Bassett had died exactly as he was purported to have, from cutting his wrists and submerging them in a tubful of warm water; she doubted Will would have a different take on it.

Pausing in her work, the girl blew away some strands of straw-colored hair that had escaped her head rag to hang in her eyes. There was something familiar about her; Nell was sure she'd seen her somewhere before, but where?

In a soft, bone-weary brogue, the maid said, "Can I help ya?"

"We understand Dr. Tanner is up here," Will said.

Eileen hesitated, then cocked her head toward a closed

door in the far wall. "He's in there." She hunkered down and resumed her scrubbing.

As they crossed the room, sidestepping Eileen and the grisly mess she was cleaning, Nell noticed some items of clothing laid out on a settee: a black, double-breasted frock coat, gray trousers, braces, socks, shirt, drawers, collar . . . The last suit of clothes Noah Bassett would ever wear.

Nell knocked softly on the door to Mr. Bassett's study.

"Miss Bassett?" Dr. Tanner said from inside.

So, Nell thought, *he even calls her that when they're alone—just as all those dour old etiquette books advised.* She opened the door.

The minister, sitting at a cylinder desk in the Spartan but sun-washed room, turned to look at them, a hint of disappointment shadowing his face when he saw that it wasn't Miriam. He rose and bowed to Nell, a ribbon-tied bundle of envelopes in his hand. "Miss Sweeney . . . Dr. Hewitt. May I . . . help you?"

"I'm just trying to get a picture of Mr. Bassett's environment and state of mind at the end," Will said.

The desk had its top rolled up. All but one of its little nooks had been emptied out onto the desktop, taking up its entire surface except for an inkstand. It was a pewter stand with two ivory-capped inkwells, an ivory-lidded stamp box, a pen rest bearing a well-used quill, and a smaller, empty rest meant for a pen knife. The lower desk drawers all stood open, the files and papers that had filled them spread out in neat stacks on the rug.

Looking from Nell and Will to the rummaged-through desk, and back again, Tanner said, "I am, of course, going through these things at Miss Bassett's behest."

"I know. I overheard." Nell was careful not to specify how very little she'd overheard, in the hope that Dr. Tanner could be finessed into disclosing what he was looking for. "Whispers," Nell said, "tend to have the unintended effect of drawing one's attention to what's being said."

"You must understand," Tanner said as he shoved his eyeglasses up, "Miss Bassett's tendency toward . . . I don't want to say secretiveness . . ."

"Circumspection?" Will supplied.

Tanner accepted the euphemism with a mordant smile. "It's the product of circumstance, not nature. She's a lady who's grown accustomed to, well, taking care of things—of *everything*—on her own hook entirely, with no aid or input from anyone else. Running a house this size with a staff that's dwindled down to one, caring for an ailing father, serving as a substitute mother to Becky after Mrs. Bassett's passing . . . It's a great deal to be laid upon one person's shoulders."

"I can understand Mr. Basset's having done little to ease her burden," Will said. "He's evidently been suffering from mental depression for years. But surely the younger Miss Bassett, as she's come of age, has been able to help out."

"Becky . . ." Tanner flipped through the letters in his hand as he composed his reply. "She's a charming girl, but she's simply never been expected to shoulder any real responsibilities."

"Are you saying she's been spoiled?" Nell asked. If so, whose fault would it be but that of the person who'd reared her—her sister Miriam?

"I wouldn't say that." Lowering his voice, his eyes

sparking with amusement over the rim of his glasses, Tanner said, "It might get back to Miss Bassett, and there'd be the Devil to pay. I say, do you mind if I, er . . ." He gestured toward the desk.

"Oh, do please carry on," Nell said. "We didn't mean to disturb you."

Acknowledging the small courtesy with a nod, the minister sat back down and placed the letters on the desk, lining them up tidily with the other piles. "Miss Bassett has found that it tends to just complicate things when she tries to share the load with Becky, what with all the explanations and instructions. And Becky, as you've no doubt observed, relishes discourse to an extent that Miss Bassett finds, well . . ."

"Time-consuming?" Nell said.

Tanner smiled. "Quite. Being a very busy lady who values her time, she's learned to keep her counsel—almost to a fault, as you've seen." Pulling a sheaf of papers from one of the cubbies, Tanner said, "In that respect, the Bassett sisters could not be more different."

Too true, Nell mused. Every thought Becky had seemed to make its way out of her mouth in short order, without benefit of any kind of filtering process.

"I imply no judgments," Tanner said as he sorted through the papers—a train schedule, a dinner invitation, an old tintype . . . "The Almighty made them both the way they are, and I daresay He loves them equally. But there's no denying they're polar opposites. Miriam took after her father. Noah was always a strong believer in personal responsibility and self-reliance."

Will said, "If Miss Bassett, the elder Miss Bassett, is

so insular, I'm surprised that she enlisted your help just now."

"As am I," Tanner said. "Surprised, but pleased. We are, after all, betrothed. It would be a sad thing, indeed, if she felt she could never turn to me." He sorted quickly through the last few items in his hand—a folded-up map, some postcards, and a yellowed newspaper clipping that made him shake his head dolefully; it was Lucy Bassett's obituary. "That's it, then," he said as he set about returning the little piles to the slots from which he'd extracted them.

"No luck?" Nell asked, even as she wondered what it was he'd been looking for.

"Not in this section here," he said, indicating the cubbies. "They're all personal papers—correspondence, memorabilia . . . Very little related to business or financial matters, and certainly nothing about his gold transactions."

His gold transactions? *Papa never talked about such matters with the family.* It had been a vague response—intentionally so, it would seem, to a direct question about whether Noah Bassett had bought gold. *He'd been melancholic for years,* Miriam had told them, by way of explaining his suicide. *Perhaps the general atmosphere of despair yesterday sent him over the edge—so many men losing everything.* "Circumspection" was one thing. It would appear she'd deliberately steered them away from the notion that her father had killed himself in despair over the gold crash. But why?

With a glance at Will, Nell asked the minister, "Was Mr. Bassett very heavily invested in gold, do you know?"

"I don't, actually. He never spoke of such things to me. Filthy lucre, and all that."

"Since his business papers are missing," Will said, "wouldn't you imagine Mr. Munro has them?"

Tanner stilled, regarding Will with a kind of guarded puzzlement. "You know about Munro?"

"That he advised Mr. Bassett on his investments?" Will said. "Yes, we know."

"He counseled quite a few gentlemen on such matters," said Nell, not wanting it to get back to Miriam that Becky had let slip this intriguing connection between the two dead men. "Word gets 'round."

Tanner let out an amused little "hmph" as he leaned over to lift a pile of papers from the floor onto the desk. "Miriam doesn't think anyone knows. She doesn't *want* anyone to know."

"Because of his . . . private life?" Will asked. "Or did she consider him a gutter-blood because he wasn't born into his fortune?"

"She's no high-hat," Tanner said as he started skimming the papers and setting them aside, "but she does hold to fairly high standards of conduct, so I suspect it's the former, though I couldn't say for sure. She's never liked to talk about him. It seemed to trouble her that he had *anything* to do with the family, but especially that he was—" He cut himself off, his brow furrowed.

"That he was what?" Will asked.

"Er, that he was . . ." Tanner shook his head without looking up. "Sorry, must have lost my train of thought. Reading and talking at the same time, you know."

Clergymen ought *to be bad liars,* Nell thought. *Otherwise, what business did they have calling themselves men of God?*

"So now that both men are dead," Will said, "Miss Bassett means to eradicate the association altogether."

Tanner frowned as he riffled through a file. "I don't know if I'd go so far as to say that."

Nell said, "She sent you to find evidence of her father's investments because she knew they would connect him to Mr. Munro, thus reflecting badly on the family. My guess is she wants to hide those papers where no one will ever find them—or destroy them." Perhaps, Nell speculated, the Bassetts' dire financial straits these past few years had made Miriam all the more determined to maintain the family's upstanding reputation—hence the need to erase the roguish Philip Munro from the picture.

"It's almost certainly what she intended," Will told Nell. "But Munro must have held on to those papers, seeing as he was acting as Mr. Bassett's agent or advisor or what have you. I'd like to take a look at them and see for myself how badly the gold failure affected Bassett's financial picture. All I need is a solid motive for suicide, and then I can move on to Munro himself—which I venture to say will prove a good deal thornier."

"Perhaps when we're done here," Nell said, "we should pay a call on Mr. Munro's sister."

"*We*," Will said with a little half-smile. "I quite like the sound of that." She must have looked flustered, because he added, "You've proven yourself quite adept in matters of deduction, and there's something about you that makes people want to open up to you."

She looked away, cheeks warming. "Dr. Tanner, I don't suppose you found a note from Mr. Bassett on his desk, or in one of those little slots. You know—a final good-bye? Some statement as to why he was taking his life?"

Tanner shook his head as he set the file aside and picked up another. "Nothing like that, and I doubt very much he'd have shoved it in one of these drawers—what would have been the point? Did you ask Miss Bassett if she found anything like that?"

Nell nodded. "She didn't." Or so she'd claimed.

WHEN they left the study, the maid Eileen was still on her hands and knees, but she'd stopped scrubbing and was gathering up the soiled rags.

"All done for now?" Will asked her.

"Got to go down to the kitchen and git some hotch-potch soup started fer dinner," she said in a soft, high-pitched voice. She was young, indeed, a waifish adolescent no more than a year or two off the boat, judging from her accent. Bracing a hand on the edge of the bed, she started pushing herself up.

Will offered her his hand, but the girl only gaped at it. Had no gentleman ever helped this poor girl to her feet?

"Allow me," he said.

"Och, ye don't want to be touchin' me, sir. I got poor Mr. Bassett's blood all over me hands."

"My own hands were covered with his blood just last night," he replied, lifting her gently to her feet despite her protestations. "I'm the surgeon who examined his body after it was brought to the hospital."

The girl couldn't disguise her revulsion. "Ya cut up

dead folks fer a livin'? Faith, I won't never grouse about me job agin."

Having gained her feet, Eileen smoothed down her humble skirts, which were hemmed above the ankle for practicality. Her left foot was shod in an ordinary, if shabby, boot, but her right . . . It didn't even look like a foot, misshapen as it was, a bulging stump encased in wood and leather.

That was when Nell realized why the maid look so familiar to her. "I say," Nell asked her, "do you attend mass at St. Stephen's—early Sunday mass?"

"Aye." That wasn't surprising; it was very much an Irish church.

Nell said, "I've seen you there." It was the girl's unwieldy, off-kilter gait that always drew Nell's attention—and pity—when the parishioners, many of them servants, lined up to receive communion. The poor girl had always struck Nell as far too young and sweet-looking to be saddled with such an affliction. "Your name is Eileen, is it not?" Nell asked.

The girl nodded. "Eileen Tierney."

"I'm Nell Sweeney, and this is Dr. William Hewitt."

Will bowed. Eileen, clearly unused to such gallantries, nodded timorously.

Nell said, "Miss Bassett tells us you were with her when she found her father's body yesterday afternoon."

She nodded morosely. "Aye, and a more terrible thing I never seen."

"What, exactly, did you see?" Will asked.

"Mr. Bassett layin' right here wid his hands in this tub, blood everywheres. Miss Bassett, she starts wailin' like a banshee."

"Did she do anything?" Nell asked.

"Just sank to her knees in that doorway there, bawlin' and screamin'. Miss Becky, she come runnin' up from downstairs. Takes one look at her da layin' there and heads straight for the jakes, like maybe she's fixin' to be sick."

"What did *you* do?"

"Nothin' at first—figgered it weren't my place—but then I seen the two of 'em wasn't gonna be good fer much, so I lifted me skirts and come on in and . . . well, once I got a look at his face, I knew he was dead and no doubt about it. He kilt himself." She executed a solemn sign of the cross. "Holy Father have mercy on him. It's a mortal sin, that is."

Will said, "You're to be commended for taking the situation in hand and going in to check on Mr. Bassett."

Eileen accepted the compliment with a shy murmur of thanks.

Nell said, "Miss Basset eventually got command of herself, I take it."

"Aye, she calmed down some, but she never did budge from that doorway."

"Did she . . . ask you to do anything?" Will asked.

The girl's gaze shifted from Will to Nell as she clutched her apron in her hands. "I'm sure I dunno what you . . ."

"To look for something," Nell prompted.

Eileen shook her head as she turned toward the door. "Weren't nothin' to find. I got to go start that hotch-potch."

"You didn't find a note?" Nell asked.

"Sorry, no," she said as she shuffled haltingly across the room.

"Eileen." Will stilled her with a hand on her shoulder.

"I told you," she said. "I didn't find—"

"Your foot," he said. "I'd like to take a look at it."

She stared at him.

"I'm a physician," Will said.

"I thought you said you was a surgeon."

"It's the same thing. If you'll just indulge me," he said as he guided her to an old horsehair wing chair, "it shan't take long, and perhaps I can even be of some help."

"There's no help fer it, and anyways, I can't afford no bone butcher." Eileen glanced at the open door and lowered her voice. "Ye know why I'm the maid of all work here, after the rest of 'em took off? It's 'cause the Bassetts can't pay nothin' but room and board no more, and ain't no one'll put up with that but me. Only reason I'm still here, doin' the work of six, is 'cause I'm a cripple, and nobody else'll have me."

"Dr. Hewitt doesn't want your money," Nell said, "and he's an excellent physician."

"Don't matter how good he is." Eileen allowed Will to ease her into the chair, but with a wary expression, as if this were some form of trickery. What Nell knew, and Eileen didn't, was that William Hewitt had always felt compelled to aid and protect the fairer sex, even back when it was he, himself, who'd been most in need of saving. "I was born this way," Eileen said. "It's God's will, that's what me mum always said."

"Is she here in Boston?" Nell asked as Will drew a matching stepstool up to the chair. Back when she'd assisted Dr. Greaves, it had been her responsibility to distract his patients with conversation so he could concentrate on his doctoring.

"Nah, Mum died when I was little. Me da saved up enough to bring us over last year, but he took sick and died on the crossing."

"I'm sorry to hear it," Nell said.

"Here." Crouching down, Will lifted Eileen's bad foot onto the stool, folded her skirt back to the knee, and studied the complicated lacings and buttons that secured her footwear—a bizarre but carefully crafted boot made of mismatched scraps of leather sewn to fit the ungainly shape beneath. "How do I, er . . ."

"I'll do it." Leaning forward, Eileen swiftly unfastened the makeshift boot and slid it off. The thick block of scarred wood that formed the sole was carved to fit her deformity and lined with sheepskin, as was the leather that surrounded the foot. Will pushed the stool right up against the chair so that Eileen's right leg, which was slightly shorter than the left, could rest comfortably on it. Even sheathed as it was in a white woolen stocking, Nell could see that her calf was withered and her foot badly malformed.

"Would you mind taking off your stocking?" Will asked.

Eileen, chewing on her lower lip, looked from Will to Nell, and then hesitantly peeled it off. She sat unmoving, the stocking twisted in her hands, as Will scrutinized her stunted and inward-bent foot, but when he reached toward it, she recoiled, crying, "Och, murther!"

"Does it hurt?" Will asked in alarm.

"No," she said, as if it were an idiotic question. "Ye said ye was just gonna look at it."

"He has to touch your foot to really tell what's wrong with it, Eileen." Nell sat on the arm of the chair and patted the girl's shoulder. "Hasn't a doctor ever examined you?"

"Doctors costs money. And what's wrong wid me is I got a clubfoot," Eileen said. "Any fool can see that."

"Yes," Will said, "but there are different variations on the condition. May I?" he asked, his hand hovering over her foot.

Nell nodded to Eileen, who looked away and muttered something that sounded like grudging permission. She sat with her face pressed against threadbare horsehair, a blush rising up her throat, as Will lifted her foot and gently manipulated it this way and that.

"Does this hurt?" he asked, sounding very much as he had while putting Nell's hair up earlier.

She shook her head.

"Does this?"

Another head shake, and another when he asked whether she ever got sores on the right side of her foot and ankle, which took all the weight when she walked.

Nell said, "I think that's what the sheepskin is for."

"It's a good boot," Will said, "as good as any physician might make."

Eileen half unburied her face, eyes sparking. "I made it meself."

"Really? Splendid job. It's kept this foot in tip-top shape. That makes you an excellent candidate for surgical repair."

"What's that?" Eileen asked. "You mean like one of them iron contraptions? I hear they hurt like the divil and don't work."

"True on both counts, especially when a clubfoot has had years to solidify, as yours has." Will rose stiffly and told Eileen she could put her stocking and boot back on, which she proceeded to do. He said, "There's a famous bone surgeon named Dr. Lewis Albert Sayre at Bellevue Hospital in New York. He's come up with a way of operating on clubfeet to untwist them and make them flat again. I understand he's had wonderful success with this surgery."

Eileen paused in the act of lacing up her boot to regard Will with undisguised horror. "You want to cut me open?"

"Not I," Will said. "I'm not qualified to perform this particular operation. But I could contact Dr. Sayre and—"

"Ain't no one gonna cut me open. I know what happens when folks get cut open, thank ye very much."

"That's all changing," Will said. "There's chloroform and ether now, to keep it from hurting, and carbolic spray to prevent—"

"Miriam!" The voice, Becky Bassett's voice, came from downstairs. *"Done already? Oh, my. That was quick."*

"That would be our cue," Will said drolly. "Here." He patted his pockets until he produced a card, which he handed to Eileen. "This is my name, and the address of my office at Harvard Medical School. If you decide you'd like to discuss the possibility of surgery, just—"

"Sure, and if I could read," said Eileen as she offered him back the card, "d'ye think I'd be on me hands and knees, scrubbin' up a dead man's blood for room and board?"

"Keep the card," Will said as he held the door open for Nell. "If you change your mind, give it to a cabman, along with some of this." He dug a generous handful of coins out of his pocket and emptied them into a startled Eileen's hand. "I'll be waiting."

Chapter 5

"I have a question about ladies' underwear," Will said as he handed Nell down from his black phaeton, parked in front of Philip Munro's house on Marlborough Street.

"Sometimes," Nell said as she stepped down onto the sidewalk, "I think you've gotten altogether too familiar with me."

"Is it customary," he asked, "as part of a lady's mourning costume, for her underclothes to be entirely black? I mean, not just petticoats and stockings, but stays, corset cover . . ."

Fluffing up her skirt, Nell said, "That's an odd question coming from a gentleman who probably knows far more than I do about the vagaries of ladies' underpinnings. And you've always professed a certain admiration for beautiful young women in mourning black—which leads me to suspect," she added with a coy smile, "that you are probably very well conversant on the subject, Dr. Hewitt."

"As it happens, *Miss Sweeney,* the last time a young widow looked upon me with favor was in England, back before the war. If memory serves me, black was reserved for the petticoats and stockings only, the rest of the undergarments being the traditional white, but it occurs to me that customs may have changed."

"Because of what you saw hanging in Miriam Bassett's drying shed," Nell said. Miriam appeared to have dyed everything but her drawers. "As far as I know, it's still only petticoats and stockings that are black, because one tends to reveal glimpses of them no matter how discreet one tries to be."

"Is it an indication of the depth of Miss Bassett's grief, do you suppose, that she's . . . surpassing convention in this regard?"

"She seems genuinely anguished," Nell said. "Perhaps she just isn't thinking clearly. Or perhaps one of her mourning dresses is so sheer that she's afraid white underclothes will show through."

"A sheer mourning dress . . ." Will mused with a wistfully salacious smile. "Now, that's an intriguing image."

"*Altogether* too familiar," Nell huffed as she turned and headed toward the house.

"I see you trying not to smile." Will hooked his arm around hers, leaning in close. "Save your ladylike outrage for the rest of the world, my sweet. I've met the actress behind the mask, and she's a damned sight more interesting than the prim and proper little Irish governess she plays."

My sweet. The endearment, offhand and lightly mocking though it was, resonated in Nell's ears as she stared up at the late Mr. Munro's imposingly tall granite townhouse. Like the houses attached to it on either side, it looked as if it had been plucked right off Paris's Champs Elysée, with its mansard roof and myriad pediments, pilasters, and balustrades. The front steps, also granite, led to a portico supported by a pair of stout Corinthian columns. This miniature pavilion formed the base of a four-story bay, crowned by the dormered attic. Every window in the house was curtained in black.

Will said, "That fourth-floor bay window, the front one—that would be the window Munro fell from. He landed on these steps."

Pointing to the ornamental molding above the portico, Nell said, "And that would be the cornice he supposedly struck on his way down. I don't see any blood or marks, though."

"Neither do I."

As they approached the front door, Nell saw that a black ribbon had been tied to the bell pull. The door was opened by a dour butler wearing a black armband, who took Will's card and sent a parlor maid upstairs to let Philip Munro's sister know that she had callers.

The reception room in which the butler left Nell and Will to wait was mournfully dim, its windows being shrouded in black and the gasolier hanging from the fourteen-foot ceiling unlit. Nell rubbed the diaphanous curtains between her fingers—silk crepe, as costly as it was fragile. The fireplace, to which Nell gravitated, was surmounted by a monumental, crepe-draped mirror, both housed in a confection of ornately carved rosewood. Among the various objets d'art cluttering the mantel was a fanciful Rococo clock of ormolu and brass, its hands stilled at just past three-forty.

Will set his hat and gloves on the marble-topped center table, pulled out a chair and gestured Nell into it, then took a seat himself.

She leaned toward him, lowering her voice so as not to be overheard by any household staff who might be lurking nearby. "Do you find it odd that Miss Munro has managed to purchase and install so much black crepe in such a short period of time? Her brother died just"—she checked her watch, which read eleven-forty—"fifteen hours ago, almost to the minute."

"How do you know exactly what time he died?" Will asked.

She nodded toward the mantel clock. "Someone obviously took note of it—a servant, most likely." It was an old custom to stop clocks at the time of death.

"That clock would indicate what time he fell from the window," Will said. "We've no idea what time he was actually killed, except that it must have been earlier than three-forty."

"Assuming you're right about his being dead before he fell."

"I am. As for the crepe, perhaps Miss Munro keeps a supply of it around for such contingencies."

"It looks brand new," she said. "Smells new, too."

"Then perhaps she sent out for it first thing this morning, or even yesterday evening, and had it installed forthwith. It could be that she's simply an extremely organized lady."

They chatted intermittently in hushed voices—mostly about what was delaying the lady of the house—until a whisper of silk drew their attention to the doorway.

For a moment, Miss Munro just hovered there, a spectral presence in the gloom. Younger than Nell had anticipated—early thirties, perhaps—she was slender and pale, a delicate china doll dressed in mourning black. She wore her hair clubbed in back and swept in two sleek black wings over her ears, the center part razor-straight. Her eyes were grayish and unremarkable, but framed by the most arresting eyebrows Nell had ever seen, as if someone had dipped a fat No. 10 brush in India ink and painted one sad black stroke over each eye.

"I'm Catherine Munro." She had a voice like feathers wrapped in velvet—throaty and drowsy-soft.

Nell rose along with Will, who bowed and said, "Good afternoon, Miss Munro. I apologize for intruding on your bereavement."

"Is it afternoon already?" Catherine Munro looked with an expression of mild curiosity toward the crepe-covered window.

"Only just," said Nell with a glance at her watch. In fact, it was ten after twelve. They'd been waiting for almost half an hour.

Will introduced them, explaining that they'd come for the purpose of investigating both Philip Munro's death and that of Noah Bassett. "There are business papers of Mr. Bassett's that his daughters are eager to reclaim. They assume those papers were in Mr. Munro's possession, given that he served as Mr. Bassett's financial advisor. As for your brother, it is incumbent upon me in my professional capacity to prove that his demise was, indeed, the result of his own doing rather than foul play."

Catherine stood looking at Will for a long moment with the same gravely placid expression she'd worn since entering the room. She had her hands clasped at her waist, bisque-white against the stark black of her dress. It was an elegantly simple mourning gown, not merely trimmed in silk crepe, like Becky's, but entirely fashioned of it, giving it an aura of lavishness despite its understated cut. The white collar and weeping cuffs—the latter nearly a foot long—were made not of muslin, but of crisp, translucent lawn. Something glinted darkly on her breast, in the center—jewelry of some sort. Her only other adornment, such as it was, appeared to be a ring of keys dangling from her belt.

When Catherine finally spoke, it wasn't to respond to Will's statement as to why he was there, but to say, "I don't suppose, Dr. Hewitt, that you are any relation to Mr. Harry Hewitt of Commonwealth Avenue."

Will paused fractionally before saying, "He's my brother." While driving over here, he'd ruminated aloud as to whether his connection to Harry would be an asset or a liability in gaining Miss Munro's cooperation. Did she loathe her late brother's notoriously loutish best friend, or had she been taken in—as had so many other women—by his looks and the devilish charm he could turn on and off at will? Now that she'd met her, Nell would bet it was the former.

"There is little family resemblance," Catherine said.

"Harry takes after our father, who, as you may know, is very fair. I enjoy my mother's coloring." In point of fact, the reason Will didn't look at all like August Hewitt was that he'd been fathered by a different man entirely, several months before his parents' marriage—a fact that had played no small part, over the years, in deepening the rift between Will and Mr. Hewitt.

"If I may say so," Catherine remarked, "you and Harry seem dissimilar in temperament, as well."

Will, apparently still unsure of the right tack, hesitated again, so Nell said, "Dr. Hewitt and his brother are as different as two men can be. It's quite remarkable to me that they share any blood at all."

Catherine shifted her gaze to Nell, her expression softening a bit. "Your name is familiar to me, Miss Sweeney. I believe I may have heard something about an engagement?"

Taken aback, Nell stammered a bit until Will rescued her by saying, "It's not official yet. As you may know, Miss Sweeney takes care of a little girl, and for now, she feels her duty to Gracie and my mother must take precedence over our marriage."

"Most commendable of you," Catherine told Nell.

The conversation felt oddly like an interview. Catherine invited them to sit and offered to ring for coffee, which Nell and Will declined.

Lowering herself into the chair Will held out for her, Catherine plucked a neatly folded cambric handkerchief from her sleeve and used it to wipe some invisible smudge from the tabletop. She seemed tired, Nell thought, heavy-lidded and a little unfocused, as if they'd awakened her from a nap, which perhaps they had.

Nell's gaze lit on the little glinting object she'd noticed before, resting on Catherine Munro's upper chest. It was a walnut-sized pendant suspended from a gold chain, comprised of scores of little faceted gems in shades of red, pink, and purple that formed a floral shape. Odd, Nell thought, that a lady as deferential to mourning customs as Catherine Munro should be seen wearing such a showy piece of jewelry the very day after her brother's death; jet or onyx would have been the conventional choice.

Catherine, having evidently noticed the direction of Nell's gaze, closed a hand around the bauble, prompting Nell to meet her eyes.

"My brother gave me this," she said in that eerily serene way of hers, "when I first joined his household twelve years ago. He'd sent for me because he needed someone— someone he could truly trust and depend on—to act as his private secretary and housekeeper. This necklace was his way of thanking me for taking on those responsibilities."

Nell wondered how Munro's business associates felt about dealing with a female secretary, but she knew better than to voice the thought.

"It's actually a sort of locket." Catherine turned the pendant over, revealing an oval-shaped, glass-covered miniature painting.

Nell leaned forward, squinting to make out the image in the semidarkness. It was a portrait of a man, brown-haired, mustachioed, and wolfishly handsome. "Is that . . ."

"Philip." Looking down at the locket, Catherine rubbed her thumb over the glass.

"So," Nell said, "you . . . commissioned Mr. Munro's portrait to fit the—"

"Oh, no, it was already in there when he gave it to me." Smiling wistfully, Catherine turned the pendant back around, patted it, and said, "I mean to wear this every day until I depart this world myself, and then I mean to be buried with it."

Nell and Will both sat back in their chairs, staring at the pendant. When the silence started to become awkward, Will said, "Er, Miss Munro, would you mind telling us how long Mr. Munro had been counseling Mr. Bassett on business matters?"

"A few months. Let's see, it would have been . . . ah, yes. Four months—since May, because that was when he first called on Mr. Bassett to offer his advice, and it was shortly after that that he and Miss Bassett . . . well . . ." She let out a long, disconsolate sigh.

Nell and Will both sat forward.

Still absently fondling the pendant, Catherine said, "I must admit, I was appalled last week, when he told me he'd actually gone and proposed to her. I told him he should give it some more time, he'd only known her four months, but he didn't want to hear it. Poor Philip. So extraordinary in so many ways, but when it came to females—especially golden little things like Rebecca Bassett—he was . . ." She shook her head, frowning grimly at the table. "As foolish as any man."

Nell said, "Your brother and Becky Bassett were engaged?"

Looking up, she said, "Well, it wasn't finalized yet, but . . . I assumed you knew. She didn't mention it when you were talking to her this morning?"

"No," Nell said. Nor had Miriam or Dr. Tanner, although it may have been what was on Tanner's mind when he said, regarding Miriam's determination to excise the memory of Philip Munro from their lives, "It seemed to trouble her that he had *anything* to do with the family, but especially that he was . . ." That he was engaged to Becky— that was undoubtedly what Tanner had started to say before he cut himself off.

Nell looked at Will, who gave her a wry shrug.

"Philip told me they couldn't make it official until they secured her father's approval," Catherine said. "But I just assumed Rebecca or the sister would have told you about it this morning, since, well . . . what would be the point of keeping it under wraps now? Philip is . . . he's gone." Her fist tightened around the pendant. "It doesn't matter anymore. Nothing can come of it now."

More bewildered than ever, Nell said, "Had they *sought* Mr. Bassett's approval?"

"Oh, yes, Philip was a gentleman—he did the proper thing. He asked Mr. Bassett for his permission, only to be summarily rebuffed."

"Really?" Nell had a hard time picturing docile old Noah Bassett having the backbone to refuse anything to a man like Philip Munro.

"I can't imagine why that should surprise you," Catherine said, a little frostily. "Men like Mr. Bassett liked to use my brother for his business acumen—and Philip, being of a generous nature, always obliged—but they never really accepted him as one of them. That was why he convinced Rebecca to keep their courtship a secret. Philip was a very astute man. He knew Mr. Bassett would never allow the likes of him to call on his precious daughter."

"Was it just generosity that prompted Mr. Munro to help

these men, or did he charge them for his services?" Will asked.

Rather archly Catherine said, "Philip was brilliant at what he did—literally brilliant, a born genius with investments. Why shouldn't he have retained a modest commission for his time and expertise?"

"No reason at all," Will said.

"It's not as if they'd ever approached him out of simple friendship, any of them," Catherine said. "They didn't invite him to dinner in their homes, never asked him along on their shooting parties, or onto their yachts, or into their private clubs. They came to him for one reason, to make money. Absurd, of course, that they should have viewed Philip as a gutter-blood just because he'd actually earned his fortune, through his own wits and hard work, instead of having it dumped in his lap. However, the fact remained that he had money, but no bloodlines. He once told me a man needed both to be a true success in this city. My goal, now that he's gone, is to make him that kind of success posthumously. I'm going to establish a charitable trust, administered by myself, of course, to do good works in Philip's name—the Philip James Munro Foundation. Generations from now, he'll be remembered and revered, long after men like Noah Bassett are gone and forgotten."

"What happened after Mr. Bassett refused to grant permission for the marriage?" Nell asked. "It must have cast a chill on his dealings with your brother."

With a bitter little huff of laughter, Catherine said, "Oh, Mr. Bassett was quick to tell Philip, right after refusing permission, that he trusted their business relationship would continue as before. It was like telling him to his face that he wasn't good enough for his daughter, but he'd appreciate it if Philip would keep making money for him. The gall! Philip was outraged at the insult, I can tell you, utterly livid. He kept it inside until he was alone with me, of course. I was the only one he could ever really unburden himself to."

Nell said, "I must say, Miss Munro, I find such blatant snobbishness a bit out of character for a man like Noah Bassett."

"Well, he was egged on by the sister, that Miriam. Philip said she had a conniption when she found out he planned to marry Rebecca. She'd been begging Rebecca all along to call it off with him, and now that they were actually engaged, she was quite beside herself. She eviscerated Philip's character—right in front of him. Mr. Bassett was there, too, and of course he got an earful, which just gave him that much more ammunition with which to turn Philip down."

"This was a week ago?" Will asked.

"Last Saturday," Catherine said. "A week ago today."

"And did Mr. Munro sever his business relationship with Mr. Bassett after that?"

Raising her gaze to the ceiling, Catherine said, "No, he did not, to my utter disgust. He told me he thought there was still a chance to get Mr. Bassett to change his mind. In fact, he'd told him as much, told all three of them. He said he wasn't the type of man to throw up his hands without bringing out every weapon in his arsenal, that sooner or later Mr. Bassett would not only allow the marriage, but give it his blessing."

"Your brother seems to have been a man who knew how to get what he wanted," Nell said. "Why didn't he just marry her without her father's permission?"

"Rebecca wouldn't hear of it—absolutely refused to go against her father's wishes—thank God. I hoped and prayed the little goose would stick to her guns and that Philip would eventually tire of the melodrama and move on."

"Because Mr. Munro and Becky had only known each other since May?" Nell asked. "Was that the sole reason you objected to the marriage?"

"I objected because there was simply no need for it." Catherine's voice remained as soft as ever, but her eyes shone like silver half-dollars in the dim light. "Why on earth should someone like Philip have had to tether himself to a wife, especially a callow little girl like Rebecca Bassett? A man like that, with his lust for life, his magnetic appeal . . . Of course he attracted females—how could he not?—but he was never the type to settle down into dreary domesticity, and why should he have had to? He had me for companionship. We've always shared a special affection, he and I, a very deep bond."

"I'm sure you were quite close," Nell said carefully, "but a gentleman does sometimes entertain a desire for a more . . . shall we say, corporeal form of female attention."

Will looked down, rubbing his mouth to hide his grin.

Straightening her back, Catherine said, "There was always . . . a certain kind of female willing to provide that sort of attention. God knows Philip didn't need to bind himself in matrimony to secure it."

Will cleared his throat, schooling his expression. "Then why did he ask Miss Bassett to marry him?"

"Were they very much in love?" Nell asked.

"In love?" With a hectic little gust of laughter, Catherine said, "It was never about *love.* Good Lord—a mopstick like Rebecca Bassett? I mean, you've met her. You've got to admit, she's a bit weak in the upper story. Philip felt nothing of the kind for her. He told me he'd never so much as kissed her. He said it was because he was trying to court her properly, like a gentleman, but I know it was really because he felt nothing for her. She's *absurd.* A *joke.* What on earth could she bring to a union with someone like Philip except for, well, being blond and buxom, which always held a certain base appeal for him. I'm sure he found her quite satisfactory in that respect, but she's terribly inane, and also terribly young, you know, *terribly* young, much too young to be considering marriage."

It had been a remarkable show of emotion, considering the languid equanimity that Catherine had displayed until now.

Will said, "Why did she consider it, then, do you suppose? Most girls of her station wait until they're in their twenties to wed."

"For his wealth, of course." She seemed calmer, but still a bit tense. "You've been inside that house. Their impecuniosity is all too evident. They've nothing left but their name. It's all they've got to trade on anymore. You asked why Philip proposed to her. It was, I believe—although he never told me in so many words—an attempt to graduate from new money to old through matrimony. Philip was famous for his unorthodox business arrangements, which was essentially what this was. As in any transaction, both parties much achieve some sort of benefit for it to work. In this case, Rebecca got rich, and Philip got to marry into one of the oldest and most respected families in Boston— even if that respectability isn't quite as . . . credible as it once was."

"Why do you say that?" Nell asked.

"Well, they're hardly as virtuous and upstanding as they'd like to make out, are they? I don't mean the father, necessarily. I barely knew him. But the daughters . . . I daresay they were a cruel disappointment to him." Catherine shook her head. "You already know what I think of Rebecca. As for Miriam, well, you must admit there's something sly and secretive about her. I always worried about Philip when I found out she'd sneaked upstairs for one of her little visits."

"Visits?" Nell said.

Chapter 6

WILL sat forward. "Miss Bassett used to visit your brother?"

Catherine sat back, idly stroking the pendant. "Quite frequently, over the past several months—clandestine little visits at night."

"Were they . . . engaged in an illicit relationship?" Nell asked.

Catherine said, "My brother never spoke to me about the women in his life. He had too much respect for me, and of course, a true gentleman is ever prudent about these things."

Perhaps, Nell thought, Philip Munro actually *had* been a gentleman in certain respects, while remaining a self-serving cad in others. Some men—women, as well—had the ability to cordon off areas of their life like that. But even if he hadn't confided in Catherine about his romantic affairs, she clearly had some of it sorted out—or thought she did.

"That said," Catherine continued, "Philip was far too much of a gentleman to have conducted a liaison of that nature with the sister of his fiancée. A love match it may not have been, but there are some lines one doesn't cross."

Will said, "Why did Miriam pay him all these visits, then?"

"I couldn't say for certain, of course, but given her virulent opposition to the marriage, perhaps she was trying to talk him into breaking the engagement."

"Do you suppose she thought your brother and Becky had feelings for each other?" Nell asked.

"Oh, good heavens, no. Miriam had known my brother for some twenty years—they used to run in the same circle. She had to know he wasn't the kind of man to lose his heart to some vacuous little blonde. Any fool could see he was just marrying her to raise his estimation in the eyes of Boston society."

"His reputation was important to him," Nell said, "Which makes me wonder if his financial reversals yesterday were very severe. That's the sort of thing that might prompt a man like him to take his life." If the gold crash had ruined Philip Munro as it had so many others, he would have been left devoid of both bloodlines and the money by which to purchase those bloodlines—a true failure by his standards.

"Philip did not take his life," Catherine said firmly.

"How do you know that?" Will asked.

"Suicide is an act of desperation and weakness," she

said. "My brother was constitutionally incapable of such an act. He was a man of backbone and vigor, a champion in everything he took on. The idea of knuckling under, to anything or anyone, was utterly repellent to him. You can't imagine how it pains me to think of his memory being sullied by the presumption that he died by his own hand simply because he was found on our front steps. You must have doubts yourself as to the cause of death, or you wouldn't be here, making these inquiries."

"I do have doubts," Will said, "but as part of an objective investigation, we need to consider the possibility that your brother might have had reason to kill himself. That's why we need to know whether he lost very much in the gold collapse yesterday."

"Philip considered his business transactions to be personal and private," Catherine said. "He never discussed them with anyone but me, ever, and of course I treated them as confidential matters. But given the situation, and the need to clear up this ugly suicide rumor, I suppose it would do no harm to tell you that Philip suffered no reversals at all yesterday."

"He lost nothing?" Will asked.

"Not a fip. I should know. I was his secretary. I was privy to all his business transactions."

"Are you sure?" Nell asked.

After a slight hesitation, Catherine said, "As of noon yesterday, he was entirely solvent." Her mouth curved in a slight smile. "My brother always liked to leave himself what he called an 'escape plan' for any transaction he entered into. That is as much as I'm willing to tell you. Suffice it to say the gold crash did not adversely affect him."

"Any thoughts, then," Nell asked, "as to why and how he died?"

Catherine said, "My feeling—and it's a very strong feeling—is that it must have had something to do with those Bassett women."

"Are you saying you think they were capable of harming your brother in some way?" Nell asked.

"Rebecca Bassett is a manipulative little gold digger under that nitwit façade, and as for Miriam, I honestly do think she's unbalanced. All those visits to my brother, her fixation on ending his engagement to Rebecca . . . To tell you the truth, she always frightened me a little. Now, she frightens me a great deal."

"How do you think he ended up on those steps?" Will asked.

"He didn't jump. Other than that, I'm at a loss."

"Perhaps we can be of some help in sorting it out," Nell said. "Would you mind our going up to his office and taking a look around?"

"I . . . don't suppose so," Catherine said. "You wouldn't be . . . moving things around, would you? I plan to leave that room and his bedroom exactly as they were when he was alive—permanently. No changes so long as I live here, which, God willing, will be for the remainder of my life."

"We'll be very careful," Will said.

"All right, then. I'll take you up there." Catherine made as if to rise, which was Will's signal to pull out her chair, then Nell's.

As Catherine ushered them out of the room, Nell said, "We *would* like to bring Mr. Bassett's private business papers back to his daughters."

"Yes, of course. Quite frankly, I'd rather not have any reminder of that family in this house."

Will said, "It would be helpful to know who came to see Mr. Munro yesterday afternoon."

"I couldn't say," Catherine said as she led them past the main staircase with its elaborately carved banisters. "I spent the morning upstairs assisting Philip with his business affairs, as I generally do, but I took to my bed around noon with a headache from the doorbell. It had been ringing all morning."

"You heard the doorbell on the fourth floor?" Nell asked.

"There are two wires on the front bell pull. One leads to a bell in the kitchen, and the other to one in the office."

Nell said, "Then I take it Mr. Munro had a great many visitors yesterday morning, if the doorbell kept ringing."

"No, it was just telegrams—scads of them. Well, one or two runners with notes asking for appointments, but mostly fellows from Western Union, delivering and picking up telegrams. I assume they had to do with the gold situation. The ringing was incessant. It gave me a beastly sick headache. I'm prone to them, I'm afraid. My lady's maid had to shake me awake to tell me . . . what happened."

"You'd been asleep that entire time?" Will asked. "Three and a half hours?"

"I'd taken a headache tonic."

"Who discovered Mr. Munro's body?" Nell asked.

"His attorney arrived for an appointment and found him on the front steps. I don't imagine he'd been there very long, or a neighbor would surely have noticed." Pausing in the doorway of a utilitarian stair hall, Catherine said,

"Philip's visitors generally came in through the back door off the kitchen yard and went up these service stairs to his office. They're the only stairs that run from the lower level, where the kitchen is, all the way up to the attic. The main staircase terminates at the third floor."

"What types of visitors did he generally have?" Nell asked.

"Oh, various sorts—the gentlemen he was partnered with in assorted ventures, friends such as your brother Harry, gentlemen he advised on business matters . . ."

"Like Noah Bassett?" Will asked.

"Mr. Bassett came occasionally, not often. I gather he was in ill health. Mostly he and Philip communicated in writing—letters delivered by messenger."

Peering up the stairwell, which was lit by a skylight, Nell asked, "What about Mr. Munro's lady friends? Other than Miriam Bassett, I mean. Did they visit him at the house?"

Catherine looked away for a moment, her mouth tight. "Some of them. Philip was generally in his office until eight or nine at night—he was a hard worker, often ate at his desk—and sometimes he would . . . entertain ladies up there."

"Did they come through the back door and up the service stairs, like the gentlemen?"

Catherine nodded. "They preferred to go unnoticed by the neighbors, as you can imagine."

Nell said, "But they can't very well have gone unnoticed by you, if you were working in your brother's office when they arrived."

"The ladies who called on my brother mostly visited in the afternoons or evenings, so I rarely saw them. If it came to my attention that Philip was entertaining one of his female acquaintances, I merely ignored the fact and went on about my business."

Discreet she might have been, Nell thought, *but not blind.* "Did they ever arrange these . . . assignations in advance?" she asked. "As your brother's secretary, I would assume you were privy to his appointments."

"That's neither here nor there, Miss Sweeney. My brother maintained an admirable discretion in such matters. So shall I." *Except, of course, when it came to Miriam Bassett,* Nell thought. "As to whether any gentlemen visited him yesterday afternoon, I believe there were several appointments on Philip's calendar, and I'd be willing to show you that page, if you'd like to see it."

"We would," Will said. "Thank you."

"You'll find most of his visitors in there, but not all," Catherine said. "Not everyone made appointments. Philip often had callers who just showed up unannounced. We can go directly up to his office, or if you'd like to know who came to see him yesterday afternoon without appointments, I can take you downstairs so you that can question our cook. She's generally the only person who would see Philip's visitors come and go—aside from Philip himself, of course." Gesturing toward the stairwell, she said, "Up or down?"

"Down," Will said.

*　　*　　*

"OH, there were a number of gentlemen come to see Mr. Munro yesterday," said Catherine's cook, a stocky Negress named Mrs. Gell, who wore a sleeveless white smock over a black-dyed dress. "A regular parade of 'em through that door there and up those stairs early in the afternoon. They'd petered out by about two."

"You were here all afternoon?" Nell asked.

"Till about a quarter past three, when I went out to do my marketing. It was close to five-thirty by the time I come back. Front steps had just been washed and there was a black ribbon on the front door. A lot can happen in a couple of hours."

The kitchen, located at the rear of the house on the ground level, had been spared any shred of black crepe, and was therefore refreshingly sunny. Its walls were brightly papered, its appointments, like the cookstove at which Mrs. Gell stood stirring a pot of custard, the very latest in design.

Turning to the scrawny, pockmarked young kitchen maid kneading pastry dough on a marble slab, Nell said, "Did *you* notice these visitors?"

"Maggie's a deaf-mute," said Catherine.

"And simple, to boot," added Mrs. Gell. "She don't notice much of anything."

Indeed, Maggie had glanced at them when they entered the kitchen, but hadn't looked up from her work since then.

"Can you tell us what any of these gentlemen looked like?" Will asked the cook.

"White men in black coats and top hats," said Mrs. Gell as she stirred.

"Mrs. Gell, if you please," Catherine said, her voice weary.

"Well, now, ma'am, I didn't turn 'round from the stove to stare at 'em, and I'm pretty sure you wouldn't have wanted me doing that if I was of a mind to. When white folks are scuttling past me like I ain't even there, not so much as a tip of the hat, which they shouldn't even be wearing indoors, much less in my kitchen, well . . . they pretty much all look the same to me." Mrs. Gell pursed her mouth, just slightly, as she hefted the custard pot from the burner.

Catherine looked down and brushed her hands over her skirt, as if sweeping off specks of invisible lint. When she was done, she stood up very straight and clasped her hands at her waist. "I shall take you upstairs."

"THIS was meant to be a bedroom when the house was built, of course," Catherine said as she showed them into the front room on the fourth floor that had served as Philip Munro's office. The windows in the bay that looked out onto Marlborough Street were quite tall, and swathed in yards of black crepe. The air was very close, and redolent of lemon oil, tobacco, and leather.

Catherine said, "The back room is a guest bedroom. In between, there's a closet, the necessary, and of course, the stairs."

"Do you mind, Miss Munro?" Stepping around a table strewn with large rolls of paper, Will pulled the crepe aside, letting sunlight stream into the room. "I'll set it right before we leave."

Nell could tell from Catherine's expression that she viewed this uncovering of her carefully draped windows as almost a form of desecration; this room was to be, after all, a sort of shrine to her sainted late brother. But she merely pressed her lips together in silent, if grim, acquiescence.

Looking around at the office, a masculine enclave of dark, glossy wood and burnished leather, Will said, "Have you spent much time up here since . . . the unfortunate incident?"

"I came up here to supervise the hanging of the crepe this morning, but I didn't touch anything, if that's what you mean."

"You didn't have one of the maids straighten up?" he asked.

Catherine shook her head. "I can't even bear the thought of dusting in here. No, everything is as it was yesterday afternoon."

"What are these?" Will asked as he flattened out one of the rolls of paper on the table. "Architect's drawings?"

Catherine nodded. "My brother was planning to build a new house out in Chestnut Hill. I take it he meant it as a sort of wedding gift for Rebecca."

"This is quite a floor plan," Will said. "How many rooms, if I may ask?"

"Twenty-eight at last count," Catherine said, "but he kept adding new ones."

"He was going to sell *this* house, then?" Nell asked.

"No, actually. His intent was to keep this house for business purposes, with me remaining here to oversee such matters for him."

Will said, "That's quite a responsible position for a lady."

"But a lonely one," Nell said. "He meant for you to live here all by yourself?"

"Of course not. The household staff would remain."

Nell wasn't quite sure how to respond to that.

"Philip . . ." Catherine began. "He . . . felt Rebecca and I might not get along. His leaving me here was meant to avoid familial discord."

"I see."

There were two desks in Munro's office—a smallish black lacquer secretary decorated with Oriental designs in gilt, and a massive, carved partner's desk which stood about five or six feet from the west wall, facing into the room. It was the secretary that Catherine unlocked with one of the keys hanging from her belt, folding down the hinged lid to produce a working surface. As with Mr. Bassett's cylinder desk, it featured an arrangement of little shelves, all neatly stocked with paper, postage stamps, sealing wax, and the like. Directly over the desk hung a brass door bell connected to a wire emanating from the wall; no wonder its ceaseless ringing had driven Catherine to her bed.

From one of the larger cubbies, Catherine slid a fancily tooled leather book with the initials PM stamped in gold on the front. "This is Philip's calendar." She opened it to the page marked with a ribbon and handed it to Will, who tilted it toward Nell: Friday, September 24th—yesterday.

Four notations were penned on the thin, ruled page, two in a jagged scrawl, and the other two in an elegant, feminine hand.

Rev. Tanner, 12:30
L. Thorpe—2:00
F. Wallace—3:30
D. Cavanaugh, 4:30

Nell and Will shared a meaningful glance. So Miriam Bassett's fiancé, Reverend Dr. John Tanner, had had an appointment with Munro yesterday afternoon.

Wrestling another key off her ring, Catherine said, "This will open the iron closet over the fireplace. That's where Philip kept all his business papers, and those of the gentlemen he advised. Mr. Bassett's papers will be there, and you may help yourself to them, but I must ask you to leave everything else as you find it."

"Of course," Nell said as she took the key.

"I pity her," Nell said after Catherine disappeared down the service stairs in a murmur of silk.

Will grunted in the affirmative as he unrolled another drawing on top of the first, weighting down the corners with four beautiful millefiori glass paperweights.

"Do you suppose it's laudanum she takes for her headaches?" Nell asked as she scanned the walls. They were covered in what looked like silk block-printed with leaves and berries, and hung with numerous framed pictures— lithographs, paintings, and a few photographs featuring scenes of hunting, horse racing, archery, and most of all, cricket.

"I suppose it's laudanum she takes just to get through each day," Will said as he perused the drawing, both arms braced on the table. "Or sleep through it. Did you notice her pupils? There was hardly any light downstairs, yet they were practically pinpoints, whereas yours"—he glanced up with a grin—"were quite fetchingly dilated. And then, of course, there was her general demeanor, the odd tranquility, the drowsiness."

There was a wooden rack on the wall behind Munro's desk that was similar to a gun rack, except that it displayed not rifles, but paddle-like wooden clubs with round handles: cricket bats. There were five of them altogether; the rack was made to hold six. Next to the rack stood a huge, ornately carved étagère, its glass shelves cluttered with silver bowls, cups, and trophies, as well as a number of gold-plated cricket balls.

Slipping the key into her chatelaine, Nell lifted one of the cricket bats off the rack. It looked old and worn, with several splits in the wood.

She said, "It amazes me that Catherine can function as she does, minding her brother's business affairs, keeping this house running . . ."

"Because of the laudanum? I doubt it's a habit of long standing, otherwise I don't imagine she'd have been able to keep up appearances as she has. And my guess is she takes just enough to make things bearable." Thumping a finger on the drawing, he said, "Take a look at this."

Still holding the bat, Nell joined him at the table. The drawing was of the grounds of Philip Munro's planned country estate, which encompassed, according to a note on the bottom, thirty-eight acres. In addition to the house, with its complex network of walks and gardens, there were fountains, two greenhouses, an orchard, a deer park, three artificial ponds, a gate house, and a carriage house several times larger than the house they were standing in.

Nell said, "Not one for half measures, was he?"

"That's the property. This is the house itself." Will rolled up the landscape plan, exposing the drawing beneath, which showed the layouts of all four floors of the mansion. It was to have been an extraordinarily complicated edifice with gabled roofs, a dozen verandahs, an oval drawing room, double ballroom, music room, conservatory, two-story library, innumerable parlors and bedchambers . . . and at the hub of it all, a majestic circular staircase.

"How must Miss Munro have felt," Nell said, "when her beloved brother, the mainstay of her life, told her he was leaving her here and moving to this . . . *castle* with the detested Becky Bassett?"

Rolling up the plan, Will said, "Possibly it was around that time that she started dosing herself with laudanum. It would have eased the hurt a bit."

"But not eliminated it altogether?" Nell asked.

"Not that kind of pain—especially if her habit is a fairly mild one. Inside, she could be seething with bitterness, even rage. What have we here?" he asked as he took the cricket bat out of Nell's hand.

"He had a sort of collection." She nodded toward the rack behind the desk.

"Those are old ones," Will observed. "Probably fairly valuable, if one is a cricket enthusiast."

"One of them is missing—assuming there were six to begin with."

"Indeed." Will hefted the bat in his hands, feeling its weight and balance. Stepping back, he gave it a slow, measured swing—not in the way one would normally swing a cricket bat, but downward from overhead.

"Could one of those have done the job, do you think?" Nell asked.

"It's heavy enough, and the shape of the edge and the toe—this bottom part here—is right to have caused those particular fractures." Will smoothed a hand thoughtfully along the blade of the bat as he carried it back to the rack and replaced it. Turning toward the desk, he said, "Fastidious, wasn't he?"

It was, Nell saw as she approached it, an austerely tidy desk. A square-shaped crystal inkwell stood in the center of the desktop, which was a flawless slab of dark-stained oak buffed to a silken sheen. In a neat row next to it were a steel pen, a mechanical pencil, and a letter opener. Aside from that, there were just three stacks of papers lined up precisely along the bottom edge; no scrawled notes, no scrap paper, no blotter, no calendar, no letters, nothing one would normally expect to see scattered across a working desktop.

Standing across the desk from Will, Nell said, "Those papers must be what he was working on when he died."

He lifted the top sheet of the middle stack and frowned, then the next, and the next, and the next, looking ever more puzzled.

"What is it?" Nell asked.

"The first page is a legal description of a piece of land in Chestnut Hill. Must be from his deed to the property he was going to build on. The two below it are stock certificates. Then come another few pages from the deed, a page from a letter someone wrote him, another page from the deed . . . It's all out of order." He riffled through the piles to either side. "These, too."

"May I?" Nell held out her hand.

Will handed the middle stack across to her, but the bottom sheet remained on the desk. When he went to lift it, it was stuck. He peeled it up by a corner, causing it to rip, a layer of it adhering to the wood, which was whitish in that area. "Looks as if there was some dampness under there."

He lifted the stack to the right, while Nell circled the desk and picked up the other one. The bottom sheets of both were likewise stuck to the desk amid a hazy water stain.

Sniffing the shred of paper in her hand, Nell said, "If I had to guess, I'd say some water spilled here, and the wood wasn't dried thoroughly enough before the papers were set back down."

Will said, "Perhaps someone was simply washing up."

"Washing a fine oak desk with water?" Nell shook her head resolutely. "It would be worth a maid's job to do such a thing. One dusts wood furniture, then oils or waxes. And this desk must have been very well cared for, because it's in perfect condition—except for these." She pointed out a smattering of dents and nicks in the section that had been marred by water.

"Yes, well, someone was also a bit careless in drying the wood."

"Careless or perhaps just in full chisel to set things right and be gone," Nell said.

Will crossed to the corner sink, a reminder that this room was originally intended as a bedroom. He lit the gas sconce on the wall above it, and inspected it closely. "No sign of blood, but a sink is easy enough to clean."

"No blood here, either, that I can see," Nell said as she scrutinized the front of the desk and then the tufted leather chair tucked into it. Pulling the chair out, she crouched down beneath the desk and examined the carpet, an Aubusson in autumnal shades of garnet and amber. "The rug is ever so slightly wet," she said.

Nell followed the damp spots across the room and around the table that held the architectural plans; the trail ended at the middle bay window. She pushed the window open as high as it would go, leaned out, and looked down onto the front steps some forty feet below. From this angle, she could see no sign of blood or damage to the cornice. It did protrude a bit from the rest of the building, but not so far as all that. A person might fall from this window without hitting it.

"Got it all sorted out, do you?" Will asked as he came up behind her. She could hear the amusement in his voice.

"I'd say you were right, it wasn't a spill," she said as she ducked back into the room and tidied her dress. "My guess is that the desk was washed with water, as well as several spots on the carpet in a path leading over here."

"A trail of blood that someone cleaned up?" Will conjectured.

"It would fit in with your theory that Munro was bludgeoned from behind, then pitched out the window."

"All right, then." Will turned and stared at the desk, his arms crossed. "Munro is sitting at his desk. He has a caller."

"Or an intruder."

"If it had been an intruder," Will said, "I can't see him just sitting there while this fellow comes 'round behind him, grabs a bat off the rack, and bashes him over the head. It had to be someone with whom he felt reasonably at ease."

"A fatal lapse in judgment."

"Munro is attacked," Will said as he crossed to the desk and sat in the leather chair. "One good whack, perhaps two, and he slumps forward"—which Will demonstrated—"onto the desk."

"And onto the *papers* on the desk."

Will sat up, nodding. "Yes, quite. His assailant rains blows upon him, several of which fracture the base and back of his skull, killing him in short order."

"And scarring the wood. Some of the blows presumably missed their mark, or slid off."

"Right." Will rubbed his fingers meditatively over the damaged wood.

"Could a wooden cricket bat really fracture something as thick and hard as a skull?" Nell asked.

"It the victim's head were supported on a firm surface, like this?" Will gave the desk a smack. "Absolutely. I've known a man to suffer a fatal skull fracture from a single punch when he was lying with his head on the ground."

"His face would have been smashed against the desk during this assault," Nell said.

"Hence the broken nose and other vital injuries to that area." Pushing the chair back, Will rose to his feet. "Our killer is left standing there with a bloody cricket bat in hand, looking at a dead man draped over the desk—or perhaps sprawled on the floor by this point. He sees the blood all over the desk and the papers and what have you, and realizes he's been witnessed coming up here, either by Mrs. Gell or that little scullery maid, whom he probably doesn't realize is incapable of identifying him. Once his butchery is discovered, it's only a matter of time before the constabulary comes knocking at his door. How to throw them off the scent?"

"Make it look like a suicide," Nell said. "The gold market has just plummeted. People will assume, as we did, that Munro was distraught over losing his investment."

The subject of the gold debacle reminded Nell about Noah Bassett's business papers. Retrieving Catherine's key from her chatelaine, she crossed to the marble fireplace in the east wall. To one side of it stood a cocktail cabinet set up with decanters and cut crystal glasses, to the other a leather-upholstered chaise lounge draped with a silken throw and heaped with pillows.

Will must have noticed her looking at the chaise, because he said, with a grin, "That would be for Mr. Munro's more . . . *corporeal* transactions, wouldn't you say?"

Countering the friendly taunt with a smirk, Nell turned and opened the cabinet doors above the fireplace, revealing the built-in cast-iron safe Catherine had mentioned.

Will said, "Rather convenient, what—gold crashing just in time to provide our killer with a motive for this trumped-up suicide?"

"Gold crashed *before* the murder," Nell reminded him as she twisted the key in the lock. "Perhaps the killer even came here planning to exploit it. Perhaps he'd loathed

Munro for some time. This was his opportunity to do him in and get away with it."

"So," Will said as he stroked a hand over the water-stained desk, "he rolls up his sleeves, heads over to the corner sink, and dampens a wash rag—his handkerchief, perhaps."

"He'd be in a hurry." Nell hauled open the door to the safe, the shelves of which were stuffed with files and papers. "Munro had a good many visitors yesterday afternoon, probably because of what was happening to gold in New York. Someone might have walked in at any moment."

"He washes up hastily, discarding or burning the bloodied papers . . ."

"If he burned them, it wasn't in this." Pointing a toe toward the fireplace, clean-swept behind a needlepoint summer screen that had probably been there for months, Nell set about emptying the contents of the safe onto the chaise, where she could inspect and categorize it.

"He takes the papers with him, then—and the wash rags and any other incriminating items, and hastily tidies up the desk. He drags Munro's body to the window," Will said, miming this as he backed up to the bay, "makes sure no one's looking, and chucks it out."

"In the course of which, some blood drips onto the carpet, requiring some more frantic housecleaning before he can slip down the service stairs and out the back door."

Will said, "If he dragged Munro's body to the window and heaved him out, there would have to have been blood on his clothing—possibly quite a bit, especially on the arms and torso area. It wouldn't have shown up on a black frock coat, not at a casual glance, but what about his shirt, above the waistcoat? How did he get away without being noticed—or did he?"

Arranging the papers from the safe into methodical stacks on the chaise, Nell said, "Munro's body was discovered at three-forty, and it couldn't have been out there on the steps for very long before his attorney spotted it, a few minutes at the most. It's safe to assume that the killer fled down the service stairs sometime before four o'clock."

"And we know Mrs. Gell was out marketing till five," Will said, "so she wouldn't have seen him leave."

"And assuming the body had already been found at that point, there would have been a great deal of commotion at the front of the house, so he wouldn't have been noticed going out the back. He could have had a buggy waiting in the alley that leads to the kitchen yards, and made it all the way home without anyone . . . Hmm . . ." Nell had opened a folder filled with small sheets of paper, all headed THE WESTERN UNION TELEGRAPH COMPANY, with messages inked on the bottom half.

"Telegrams?" Will said.

Nell nodded. "All from New York City, and all dated . . ." She finished leafing through the stack. "Yes, every one dated September twenty-fourth. Yesterday."

"How many?" Will asked.

"Thirty, exactly," Nell said as she finished counting them. "They've been stacked in the order in which they were received. The bottom one came in at eleven oh-nine in the morning, the top one . . . eleven thirty-nine."

"Thirty telegrams in as many minutes," Will said. "That *is* curious."

"Most of them are like this one." Reading from a telegram in the middle of the stack, she said, " 'To Mr. Philip Munro, eleven nineteen A.M. Confirm twelve-hundred ounces sold at one-sixty per at eleven fifteen today. Yield one hundred ninety-two thousand.' It's from William Heath and Company."

"That's a brokerage house."

"I'm surprised you know that," Nell said.

With a grin, he said, "You don't think I keep *all* my money stuffed into that raggedy old doctor's bag."

"Of course not," she said, although she had, actually. Flipping through the telegrams, she said, "It would appear that Mr. Munro sold millions of dollars' worth of gold yesterday—six or seven million, maybe more—through a number of different brokers, all before noon . . ."

"When its value would have plummeted." Dryly Will added, "How very fortuitous."

"He also sold quite a bit on behalf of other investors. I recognize most of the names. Davis Cavanaugh, Horace Bacon, Phineas Ladd, Leo Thorpe, Orville Pratt . . . All men who move in your parents' social circle."

"Not surprising," Will said. "Any mention of—"

"Noah Bassett? None. Perhaps he hadn't invested in gold." She skimmed the telegram at the very bottom of the stack, which was recorded in Boston at 11:09 A.M. "This is the first one he received yesterday morning. It was sent from Washington, D.C., not from New York. 'To Mr. Philip Munro. Been reading classic verse and thought of you. To wit—Burns' "To a Mouse," seventh stanza, and Dame Prudence's proverb in Chaucer's "Melibee." Praemonitus, praemunitus, my friend. G.B.' " Looking up, she said, "My Latin's not what it could be."

"Praemonitus, praemunitus," Will said. "Forewarned is forearmed."

"Interesting."

"Quite." He came over and took the telegram from her. "The first reference is to a Robert Burns poem—'To a Mouse, on Turning Her Up in Her Nest with the Plough.' I had it committed to memory when I was around fourteen, along with about a hundred other poems."

"Good heavens," Nell said as she continued sorting the contents of the safe.

"They're dreadfully keen on that sort of thing at English boarding schools. Burns was always a tough nut to memorize, because he wrote in Scottish dialect. God, how I detested him at the time. Years later, when I was at Edinburgh, I actually grew quite fond of his work, perhaps because I'd picked up a bit of the culture and vernacular, and had a better understanding of what he was really saying."

"Do you remember any of this 'Mouse' poem?" she asked.

Folding his arms, Will settled his long body into that distinctive hip-shot stance of his and looked toward the window, as if gazing at something in the far, far distance. In a deeply soft, undulating Scottish burr, he said, " 'Wee, sleeket, cowran, tim'rous beastie, O, what panic's in thy breastie . . . ' "

Nell smiled, not just at Burns's image of a cowering little mouse, but at Will's unexpectedly earnest recitation.

" 'Thou need na start awa sae hasty, Wi' bickering brattle. I wad be laith to rin an' chase thee, Wi' murd' ring pattle.' " Will paused, as if concentrating. "Then comes an apology for man's dominion and, let's see, something about the mouse being an earth-born companion and fellow mortal . . ."

"Sounds lovely."

"It is, actually. I can't remember the middle bits, just the beginning and end. There were eight stanzas, as I recall, so the seventh would have begun . . ." He frowned at the carpet, rubbing his chin. " 'But Mousie, thou are no thy-lane, In proving foresight may be vain. The best laid schemes o' Mice an' Men, Gang aft agley, An' lea'e us nought but grief an' pain, For promis'd joy.' "

" 'The best laid schemes,' " she said. "That's from this poem?"

He nodded. "In the Queen's English, it would be 'The best laid schemes of mice and men oft go awry, and leave us nothing but grief and pain for promised joy.' "

" 'The best laid schemes oft go awry . . .' " Nell murmured.

" 'Forwarned,' " Will said, " 'forearmed' . . ."

". . . 'My friend.' "

"Whereupon he promptly sold millions of dollars of his own gold, plus whatever he'd purchased on behalf of his . . . I suppose one would call them clients. He did take a commission." Lifting the telegram, Will read the name at the bottom. "G.B. Ring any bells? You're more in tune with Munro's social circle than I."

Nell shook her head as she pulled a stack of leather folios from the safe. "There's no one I can think of with those initials, and anyway, I only know the people here in Boston. That telegram was sent from Washington."

"Forewarned," Will said, "that something had gone awry?"

"Some 'best laid scheme,'" Nell said as she skimmed the contents of the folios, each of which contained documents related to a different gentleman's investments. "So it would seem."

"If this telegram is, indeed, a veiled message, then it would appear we've deciphered part of it. I'd give my right arm to be able to quote Dame Prudence's proverb from the *Tale of Melibee,* just to see you gazing up at me with astonished admiration, but I'm afraid that particular piece wasn't on the memorization list at Eton. It's one of the *Canterbury Tales.*"

"I know," Nell said. "I've read them, but I can't recall anything about a proverb. Ah-hah," she said as she withdrew from a fat green folio a sheaf of correspondence held together with a straight pin.

"Pay dirt?"

"Letters from Mr. Bassett to Philip Munro, beginning"— she checked the date of the bottom letter—"May twenty-first of this year. Do you want to take a look at these while I see what else is in here?"

Will took the letters from her and sat at the foot of the chaise to peruse them.

Nell flipped through a stack of documentation relating to Noah Bassett's business dealings until she came to a promissory note, which she unfolded and read. "Mr. Bassett took a loan of fifty thousand dollars from the Tenth National Bank on the seventeenth of June, using his house as collateral."

"It was apparently at Munro's urging," said Will as he thumbed through the correspondence. "This is from Bassett's second letter to him. 'I beseech you, Philip, do consider to whom you are dispensing this counsel. If I'd the wherewithal to invest as you've advised, I should never have found myself in a state of such abject pecuniary embarrassment.' Then, a couple of weeks later . . . let's see, here it is. 'If, as you insist, it is the only way to regain my financial footing, I shall borrow against the house so as to invest as you see fit. It need hardly be said that I do so with a great many misgivings, which I shall set aside in deference to your savoir faire in matters of a fiscal nature. With humble gratitude for your assistance, and trust in your good judgment, I remain yours respectfully, Noah Bassett.' "

"Listen to this," Nell said as she read from a handwritten document, signed, witnessed, and notarized. " 'To all persons, be it known that I, Noah Zachariah Bassett of Mount Vernon Avenue, Boston, Massachusetts, have made and appointed, and by these presents do make and appoint, Philip James Munro of Marlborough Street, Boston, Massachusetts, my true and lawful Attorney-in-Fact. I hereby grant said attorney full power and authority to do and perform all and every act and thing whatsoever necessary to be done in order to carry on any business transaction of any kind of which I am now or hereinafter may become interested, including opening, changing, or closing accounts, making deposits and withdrawals, signing receipts, and entering into any transaction relating to any investments with or through banks, insurance companies, stock brokers, or other like institutions, and to execute such instruments in writing of whatever kind and nature as may be necessary and proper in the exercise of the rights and powers herein granted. In witness whereof, I have hereunto set my hand and seal this seventeenth day of June, eighteen sixty-nine.'" Looking up, Nell said, "The same date that he borrowed that fifty thousand dollars."

"Quite a sweeping letter of attorney," Will said. "It gave Munro the legal right to do just about anything he wanted with Bassett's fifty grand—on Bassett's behalf, of course, but without his needing to sign anything or even be aware of the business being transacted in his name. Munro probably insisted on it."

"Poor Mr. Bassett." His signature, Nell saw, had been painstakingly penned, but it still had a quivery, rheumatic look to it. Setting it aside, she withdrew the last item in the folio, a pack of five heavy envelopes, each a slightly different color, tied together with string. She untied them and slid a trifolded document out of the top one.

"What have you got there?" Will asked.

"A certificate of some sort. No, an insurance policy, life insurance from"—she checked the flowery lettering on the face of the policy—"the New England Mutual Life Insurance Company. Mr. Bassett took it out on himself in . . . let's see . . . November of eighteen forty-nine. Almost twenty years ago."

"In what amount?" Will rose from the chaise to peer over her shoulder.

"Twenty thousand dollars."

"That's generally the limit on such policies," Will said.

The other four envelopes housed polices on Mr. Bassett in the same amount, issued in November and December of

1849 by Mutual Life of New York, Connecticut Mutual Life, Empire Mutual Life, and the Equitable Life Assurance Society of the United States. Lucy Bassett was named as the beneficiary on all of them.

"That's a hundred thousand dollars in life insurance," Will said, "payable, I would assume, to Miriam and Becky Bassett now that Mrs. Bassett and the son are dead."

Nell finished emptying the safe, but found only one more item of interest: another sheaf of telegrams in a folder labeled GOLD, which documented Munro's purchases on behalf of himself and the gentlemen he represented, all of which took place over the past two months. One of those gentlemen was Noah Bassett, who on the twenty-second of June—just a few days after signing that note and letter of attorney—bought 350 ounces of gold at $142 an ounce, for a total purchase price of $49,700.

"Munro invested Bassett's entire loan proceeds in gold," Nell said.

"And left him holding it at noon yesterday, despite having evidently been warned that its value was about to plummet."

While Nell returned the papers to the safe, Will gathered together the correspondence, insurance policies, and other documentation relating to Noah Bassett, and stuffed them back in the green folio. "I'll take a closer look at these this evening," he said, "and then we can give them back to his daughters."

"You'd best take the telegrams, too," Nell said. "Both sets."

"You do realize that would be stealing," Will said.

"As a former expert on the subject, I can assure you a

thing's not stolen, per se, so long as you give it back. Eventually."

"Munro, you lazy wanker!" It was a man's voice, a familiar one, rising from the stairwell to the accompaniment of fast-pounding footsteps.

Nell looked toward Will, who grimaced, having recognized his brother's voice.

"I've been waiting on my front stoop for half an hour," bellowed Harry Hewitt as he bounded into the room, cricket bat in hand, "Where the hell have you . . ."

Harry's careless grin faded as his gaze shifted from Nell to Will, and back again. With a look of disgust, he greeted her with his customary, "Shit."

Chapter 7

WILL responded to his brother's vulgarity as he always did, with a low, menacing, "There's a lady present, old man."

Harry sneered at Nell, but said nothing. A handsome devil, more so than ever with his skin and hair newly gilded by the sun, he sported but two physical imperfections: a small scar that made his left eyelid sag ever so slightly, and a bulge just below the bridge of his nose. The former was dealt to him by Nell, the latter by Will on her behalf; every time the narcissistic Harry Hewitt looked in the mirror, he would be reminded anew how much he loathed his mother's upstart Irish governess and the elder brother who was presumably courting her. He'd grown a small moustache since she'd last seen him, much like that of Philip Munro in the little portrait Catherine wore around her neck.

A born dandy, the "Beau Brummel of Boston" was as stylishly attired for his cricket match as for any other social engagement. His flannel trousers, shin pads, and shirt were as spotlessly white as if they'd never been worn. In lieu of a belt, he wore a scarf emblazoned with the same blue and yellow stripes as his necktie, jacket, and cap. It was an odd cap, brimless, like a Chinaman's, and ringed with those gaudy stripes. He undoubtedly thought it quite sporty and dashing, never mind that Nell couldn't even look at him for fear of laughing in his face.

She was saved such an outburst by Will, who snatched the cap off Harry's head and thrust it in his brother's free hand. "You've got the manners of a ditchdigger, Harry."

Actually, he didn't, when it suited him. From all accounts, Harry could act the perfect gentleman if he wanted to dazzle some naïve mill girl or smooth-talk the proprietor of a gaming hell into taking his I.O.U.

"What are you two doing here?" Harry asked as he swept his gaze around the room. "Where's Phil? They'll be waiting for us up at the Peabody Club."

Despite the sneer, despite the hat, and most of all despite what he'd done to her—or tried to do—last year, Nell couldn't suppress a pinch of pity as she watched Harry look around like a puppy searching for his beloved master.

He would have barged in through the back door and up the service stairs without so much as a glance in the direction of Mrs. Gell, who might have told her about Munro if he'd bothered to tip that ridiculous hat in her direction.

Will glanced at Nell as if for moral support, then started to say something, only to sigh and rub his neck. "Harry . . . Curse it, man. Don't you read the papers?"

"I only just woke up an hour ago, and when I looked at the clock, it was all I could do to get myself dressed and presentable before Phil came to collect me for our match. Every Saturday afternoon, we play against . . ." He trailed off, looking back and forth between Nell and Will. If she appeared half as somber as he did, Harry had to know something was seriously amiss.

Will said, "I'm afraid I've some bad news for you, old man—really bad news."

Harry just stared at his brother, his eyes glassy and a little too fixed, the hat clutched in one hand, bat in the other.

Nell turned away, crossed to the window, and gazed out at the houses across the street, wishing she were somewhere else, anywhere but here.

Quietly Will said, "There was an . . . incident, yesterday afternoon. Munro . . . he was found out there on the front steps. It would appear—"

"*What?* What do you mean, 'he was found'? Is he hurt? Sick?"

"He fell from that window," Will said. "I'm sorry, Harry. He's dead."

There came a pause of several long seconds, then Harry said, "You son of a bitch, what are you trying to—"

"Harry, you need to listen to—"

"And you need to kiss my ass. I don't know what you're trying to—"

"He's dead, Harry. I autopsied him myself."

"*Liar!* You're a goddamn liar! He can't have just fallen from that window. Look at it! You'd have to *climb out* of the damn thing. You couldn't just *fall.*"

Nell leaned on the windowsill and closed her eyes,

wishing she could close her ears to Harry's pain, because it was the last thing she wanted to hear. Not that it should trouble her; she should revel in it, after what he'd done to her. But she wasn't made that way, nor did she care to be.

In a voice shaky with emotion, Harry said, "This has something to do with that uppity little bit of cheap Irish lace over there. She put you up to—"

"Harry," Will growled in his warning tone.

"She's got your cherry splitter in a vise, you know that, don't you? She's just leading you around by your—"

Nell cringed at the sound of Will's fist striking his brother's face, squeezed her eyes shut as Harry landed with a grunt and a torrent of curses on the carpeted floor.

"My sympathy only extends so far," Will said in a softly strained voice. "You will leave Miss Sweeney out of this conversation."

Harry muttered something unintelligible, his breath coming in tremulous pants. He sniffed, coughed, sniffed again.

Nell turned to find him sitting up on the floor, holding a handkerchief to the side of his mouth. His tawny hair hung over his forehead, and his left cheek bore a scrape surrounded by a livid bruise. He tried to glare at her, but his eyes were wet and his face blood-flushed, which somewhat compromised the effect.

Will met Nell's gaze with a wretched expression; this was no easier for him than for her.

Sitting Indian-style on the floor, Harry dug an engraved silver flask from inside his coat and unscrewed it one-handed, which looked to be a practiced maneuver. Removing the bloodstained handkerchief from his mouth, he tilted the flask and took a long pull, wincing at the sting of alcohol on his split lip. Harry gulped as if it were water, his hand trembling. He wiped his mouth with the handkerchief, gasping, then raised the flask again and emptied it.

He shook his head as he screwed the top back on the flask. "What happened?" he rasped.

Will said, "The police think he committed suicide."

"Mullet-headed pigs," Harry muttered as he dabbed the handkerchief on his mouth, his gaze unfocused. His voice seemed a little thick-tongued; the drink, perhaps, or his swollen mouth, or perhaps both. "Why would a man like Phil Munro kill himself? He had everything. He was . . ." He ducked his head, the bloody handkerchief pressed to his mouth, his shoulders quaking.

Nell wrapped her arms around herself and looked down.

Will said his brother's name softly.

Harry's muffled sobs were excruciating to listen to.

"Harry." Will hiked up his trousers and crouched next to his brother. "Harry, I'm sorry for your—"

"Go to hell!" Harry lashed out with his fists, catching Will on the side of the head. He grabbed his cricket bat and leapt to his feet. "You're not sorry for anything!"

He swung the bat as Will was rising; Will ducked before it could connect. "Harry, for pity's sake!"

Harry spun around and whipped the bat across the big oak desk, sweeping papers across the room, along with the crystal inkwell, which cracked against the wall, splattering ink all over the luxurious silk wallpaper.

"Harry!" Will yelled as he gained his feet.

Nell backed up swiftly as Harry took the bat to the étagère, shattering the glass shelves as he sent Munro's cricket trophies flying. "Don't you tell me you're sorry, damn you!" he screamed as he smashed the glass on a row of framed prints. "You're not—"

"Stop this!" Will grabbed the bat as Harry raised it overhead, wresting it from his grip. "For God's sake, Harry."

"Stop telling me what to do!" Red-faced and wild-eyed, Harry wheeled toward the table with the architectural drawings as Nell stumbled out of his way. He seized a rolled-up plan and tore it in half, then grabbed one of the paperweights and hurled it at his brother.

Will sidestepped the glass sphere, bunting it away rather deftly with the bat as Harry closed his fist around another.

"Oh, my God."

Harry stilled at the faint words from the doorway, the paperweight raised to throw. Catherine Munro, pale as chalk, stood with her hands clasped at her throat, surveying the carnage Harry had made of the room she'd meant to keep forever untouched. "Oh, dear God." She closed one hand around the locket housing her late brother's portrait, the other over her mouth.

Harry stared at her, wet-faced, his chest pumping, a trickle of blood coursing down his chin from the split lip. He blinked at Catherine, then at the room around him. He seemed to wilt; the paperweight thudded onto the floor.

"Miss Munro . . ." Nell began. As she was pondering what to say next, Harry bolted across the room, muscled Catherine aside, and tore down the stairwell, his footsteps reverberating through the house.

* * *

"THERE he is." Will, walking arm in arm with Nell in the Public Garden, pointed to the far side of the lake, where a lone figure sat slumped over on a bench, elbows on knees. From this distance, Nell would have taken him for an old man, were it not for that garishly striped jacket.

After Harry's abrupt departure, she'd watched from the window of Munro's office as he jogged east on Marlborough Street. He slowed down as he approached the park. Harry had always liked the Public Garden, Will had said. Idyllic in the manner of an English country estate, it was one of his favorite trysting places.

Harry lifted his head as they approached, squinting against the midday sunshine. His posture remained the same, as did his expression of drained resignation. He was hatless, his well-oiled hair in disarray, a crust of blood drying on his lower lip, that abraded bruise on his cheekbone purpling already.

He offered no objection when Will sat beside him on the bench. Nell, knowing better than to force him to interact with her, chose the next bench over—close enough to hear what was said, but far enough away so that Harry could dismiss her from his mind if he chose to.

From inside his morning coat, Will retrieved his own flask, which was oval-shaped and about half the size of Harry's, and offered it to his brother. "Brandy," Will said. "Not your poison of choice, I know, but . . ."

Harry took it and sat upright to swallow its contents in a single tilt. He returned it to Will, sat back, and scrubbed his hands over his face, flinching when he touched the contusion on his cheek.

"Sorry about that," Will said, "but you were begging for it."

Harry just stared, rheumy-eyed, at the breeze-riffled surface of the water. A young nursemaid was wheeling a perambulator down the walk that surrounded the lake; otherwise, this area of the park was remarkably empty for such a fine, sunny day. He felt around inside his coat, muttered something under his breath, and said wearily, "Forgot my cigars."

Will pulled a tin of Bull Durhams from his coat and flipped it open. "Just don't let the gendarmes catch you smoking out here."

Harry slid a cigarette out of the tin and looked at it. "You have the nerve to call *me* a ditchdigger?" Indeed, when Nell first met William Hewitt a year and a half ago, he was the only wellborn gentleman she'd ever seen with a cigarette in his hand.

Will took out his match safe and lit his brother's cigarette. He didn't take one himself, which surprised Nell. If any situation called for an "inhalable nerve tonic," it seemed to her it would be this one.

Harry drew on the cigarette, gagging. "Tastes like shit."

Will's gaze flicked in Nell's direction. Knowing his instinct would be to upbraid his brother for swearing in her presence, she caught his eye and shook her head. It was better that she should remain on the periphery—seen from the corner of Harry's eye, perhaps, but not heard.

"It's probably stale," Will said. "I've been carrying that tin around for a while."

Harry smoked the cigarette down to a stub, asked for

another, and lit it off the first. "So, what *were* you doing at Phil's?" he asked.

"Trying to figure out how he died."

"I thought you said he killed himself."

"The police said he killed himself. He didn't."

Harry turned to look at his brother for the first time.

Will said, "He was attacked from behind, possibly with one of his own antique cricket mallets. The cause of death was a fractured skull. His assailant then pitched him out the window to make it look like suicide."

Harry returned his gaze to the lake, puffing thoughtfully on the cigarette. "I knew he couldn't have . . ." He shook his head. "Not a man like that. Never."

"At first, we thought he might have been ruined when gold collapsed, but that's not the case. We know he bought millions of dollars' worth of it over the summer, when it was a bull market, on behalf of himself and the men he advised. But he dumped it yesterday morning, right before word arrived in the Gold Room that President Grant would be selling four million in federal gold, which was when all hell broke loose."

"And when everyone else who owned gold got trounced," Harry said. "He's a clever bastard. Was. Must have made a pretty penny yesterday."

Not so Noah Bassett, whose $50,000 in borrowed money went to buy gold that Munro chose not to sell, leaving the poor old fellow ruined—a wrinkle that Will wisely chose to withhold from his brother at the present time.

"If I'm to prove Munro was murdered," Will said,

"I need information. That's why I was in his office. And that's why I'd like to talk to you. You were his best friend. You might know things about him that others didn't."

Harry took a long draw on the cigarette. "I don't like people thinking he did away with himself." He tapped his ash onto the ground; some of it fell onto his pristine white shin guard, but he didn't seem aware of it. "What do you want to know?"

"I'm intrigued by his connection with the Bassett family," Will said, "especially given that Noah Bassett was also found dead yesterday."

"Yes? Well, he'd been ailing, hadn't he?"

"It was suicide," Will said. "There was no note, but he was ruined in the gold crash, so that would appear to provide a motive. What I'm most curious about is Munro's relationship with Bassett's daughters."

"He was engaged to the one and amusing himself with the other," Harry said matter-of-factly.

"Amusing himself?" Will asked. "Are you saying Miriam Bassett was Munro's mistress?"

"God, no, he already had one of those. And a Brahmin princess like Miriam, impoverished or no, would never stoop to being a mistress if she thought she could sugar-talk the fellow into marrying her."

"But she already has a fiancée," Will said. "He's a minister, one of Martin's professors at Harvard."

"You don't say. Well, perhaps she was just keeping the good reverend in reserve—a contingency plan in case she couldn't manage to bring Phil around. Not that she had a prayer of doing that, of course. She was nothing to him but a sort of . . . diverting nuisance."

"So, when you say Munro was 'amusing himself' with her, that means . . ."

"Trying to crawl under her petticoats, and giving it quite the heroic effort, for all the good it did him. Other women, they'd tumble pretty fast for Phil, but Miriam wouldn't give an inch. Normally he didn't have a lot of patience for the lovesick prigs, used to flick them away and move on to likelier prospects. But he told me Miriam just refused to be gotten rid of, kept after him all summer, but with those legs locked in the closed position, which made her something of a challenge."

"Kept after him?"

"Hounded him—that's how Phil put it. Mostly it was little surprise visits in the evenings. Women did tend to go dotty over him, and they could become tiresome. In Miriam's case, I suppose his reasoning was that if he couldn't be rid of her, he may as well try to get his corn ground—so long as he could do so without any mawkish declarations or promises, of course. *He* was engaged, too, you know."

Ah, yes, his unofficial betrothal to Becky Bassett. Had Catherine Munro actually believed what she'd said about her brother being too much of a gentleman to have carnal designs on his fiancée's sister? *A love match it may not have been, but there are some lines one doesn't cross.*

"It didn't give him pause," Will asked, "trying to cold-heartedly seduce his prospective sister-in-law?"

Harry grinned. "The willie doesn't have much of a con-science, brother—and if ever there was a town bull, it was Phil Munro." Almost reverently he added, "Most horn-mad fellow I ever knew."

"Did he actually tell you all this, about Miriam?" Will asked.

Harry squinted into the smoke as he inhaled. "What he told me was that it was really getting to him, her holding out so stubbornly against all his smoothest maneuvers. He told me it wasn't so much that he wanted her, although he did, desperately. He wanted her to want *him*—and to tell him as much. It wasn't enough for her to just submit, not after all the waiting and all the effort he'd gone to. She had to ask for it—better yet, beg."

Will said, "Are you sure he wasn't just telling you all this to enhance his reputation as a lothario?"

"I know she used to pay him those covert little nocturnal visits," Harry said. "A few nights ago—Wednesday, I think it was—I caught her slipping out the back door of his house. I was stopping by to see if Phil wanted to pay a visit to that swanky new jay house over on Bowdoin—Flora's. You ever been there?"

"No."

Harry snorted on a gust of cigarette smoke. "Wouldn't admit it if you had, would you? Not in front of *her.*" He cocked his head toward Nell, whom he'd apparently tired of pretending to ignore. Now, it would appear, he was going to do his best to shock her.

"They've got the freshest meat in Boston at Flora's," Harry said, "sweetest little chickens you ever pegged. Phil and I used to pick out two and get a room with a nice, big bed and have us a little buff-ball. They know how to take it rough there, and they aren't stingy with the absinthe, either."

Will, obviously loath to chastise Harry lest he get up and walk away, merely closed his eyes and rubbed the bridge of his nose. His ears, Nell noticed with some amusement, had turned a scalding purplish red.

For his part, Harry seemed to have put his anguish behind him, or nearly so. He'd always had an almost indecently resilient temperament; his tribulations tended to be short-lived.

"If it was nighttime," Will asked, "how are you sure it was Miriam Bassett you saw?"

"There was a lamp in the kitchen window, so I got a pretty good look at her." Harry sat back and crossed his legs. "I hid behind the coal shed while she crossed the kitchen yard. She kept looking 'round to make sure nobody saw her."

"I take it she didn't see you," Will said.

"She wouldn't have, if I hadn't stepped out from behind the coal shed and tipped my hat to her," Harry said with a snigger as he crushed the spent cigarette underfoot. "You should have seen her mouth drop open. She turned and fled like I was Frankenstein's monster. I went in the house and up the service stairs, and when I get to the third-floor landing, who do I see on her way down, but that sister of his."

"Catherine?"

"She didn't see me, 'cause she'd turned to scream at Phil, who was still up in his office."

"She was *screaming* at him?"

"Oh, she was fit to be tied—crying, wailing . . . 'You can't do this! It's unspeakable!' "

"Can't do what?" Will asked.

Harry shrugged. "Carry on with Miriam, I assume. My best guess is that she walked in on them and realized Phil was trying to seduce his fiancée's sister. She's a demon for propriety, you know, always worried about Phil fitting in with 'the right sort.' "

"Was there any response from Phil to her outburst?"

"He came to the top of the stairs and saw me, which was when Catherine realized I was there. She started screaming at *me*, then—accused me of eavesdropping, called me all sorts of things. Phil very calmly told her to go to her room and take some of her medicine and lie down." With a salacious grin, Harry said, "I should have lain down with her and given her some of the medicine she *really* needed. Those frustrated old maids, they're aching for it, you know—they just don't realize it. Turns them into raving bedlamites."

Will caught Nell's gaze. She rolled her eyes.

"I wasn't sure Phil would be interested in a visit to Flora's after that," Harry said, "but he said he hadn't gotten any in two days, so he was overdue for a poke. We had a damned fine time that night—*damned* fine."

"So, in addition to his . . . amusement with Miss Bassett," Will said, "Munro frequented the houses of assignation and had a mistress. Were there other lady friends that you knew of?"

"Scores, but they weren't really ladies, and they weren't really friends, and it never lasted beyond a tumble or two."

"Who was the mistress?"

"Sophie Wallace, of course."

Will cocked his head, as if seeking elaboration.

"Sophie Wallace," Harry said. "Everybody knows about Phil and Sophie."

"Since I clearly don't, perhaps you'll enlighten me."

"Oh, she's a juicy little peach, very blond, very voluptuous." Leaning his head back, Harry ran his hands over his hair, slicking it into a semblance of the pomaded perfection it had been when he left the house an hour ago. "Light in the tail, of course, a real tart, but not your run-of-the-mill baggage. Quite well born, really. Her father was a Cabot—a lesser branch of the family, but a Cabot nonetheless. What I mean to say is, she's from *people,* not just some . . ."

"Some tart from some other branch of the animal kingdom?"

"Granted, she's getting a bit long in the tooth—she's forty if she's a day—but still quite the dame. Always on heat, or with that look in her eye, if you know what I mean. A tigress in silk stockings. I swear, I thought Phil had about a hundred screws loose when he let that one slip the leash."

Harry clasped his hands behind his head and propped an ankle on his knee, only to notice the dusting of cigarette ash on his otherwise immaculate white shin pad. *"Shit."* He tried to brush it away, but of course, that only turned it into a grayish smear. "Damn it all, these were brand new. Never even wore them in a match, and now I'll have to toss them."

"Can't you have the laundress bleach it?" Will asked.

"It'll never look the same," Harry groused as he rubbed at the spot. *"Damn."*

With a bemused little half-smile in Nell's direction, Will said, "Tell me, Harry, when was it Phil ended things with Miss Wallace? Was it recently?"

"It's *Mrs.* Wallace, and it was just last week." Harry gave up rubbing the ash and sat back to pout at the stain. "Damn."

"*Mrs.* Wallace? Is she a widow?"

"Married. The cuckold in question is Freddie Wallace, Phil's attorney."

F. Wallace—3:30

That was why the name "Wallace" had seemed so familiar to Nell. *His attorney arrived for an appointment and found him on the front steps.*

"Cuckold?" Will said. "Does Mr. Wallace know about his wife and Munro?"

"He didn't for the longest time, never mind that it had been an open secret for years—decades, really. They tell me Phil had been banging her since his freshman year at Harvard. Sophie was a year or two older, but no blushing maiden. I hear they met when he walked into a professor's office and found her bent over the desk. She was unwed at the time—didn't marry Wallace till she was almost thirty. Got tired of waiting for Phil to ask her—that's what I heard—and Wallace was damnably persistent with his proposals. He adored her, worshipped her like a goddess."

Will said, "And yet, the entire time she was married to Wallace, she continued serving as Munro's mistress?"

"That right, and Wallace, the poor lovesick mutt, didn't suspect a thing till a couple of weeks ago, when he came home and found a diamond and bloodstone tiepin on Sophie's night table that he recognized as Phil's. I heard he walked away from the house in tears, clutching the damned thing—literally walked down the street that way. He moved into the Parker House and initiated divorce proceedings."

"Mrs. Wallace lost a husband and a lover in fairly short order," Will said. "It would have been about a week later that Munro ended things with her. Was it because of his engagement to Miss Bassett?"

On a little grunt of laughter, Harry said, "A man's engagement doesn't eliminate his need to shake the sheets now and again—I should know. If anything, one tries to get in as much as possible before the wedding, because afterward, one has to sneak about for one's sport." With a derisive little sneer, he added, "A married man is expected to be *discreet*, don't you know."

Harry asked for another cigarette; Will, of course, obliged.

"Did Wallace ever confront Munro?" Will glanced at Nell as he asked the question; it would seem he recalled the three-thirty appointment, as well.

"Oh, yes," Harry said through a cloud of smoke, "and a most entertaining spectacle it was. Wallace made quite an ass of himself in the dining room of the Parker House night before last."

"Thursday?" Will said. "What did he do?"

"He barged in and stumbled over to our table—Phil and I were having dinner with Larry Pinch and Ezra Chapman. Anyway, Wallace lit in on Phil, very loudly and crudely, in front of the entire dining room. He was drunk as a lord, of course, could barely stand. Accused Phil—his most important client, mind you, the one who pays the lion's share of his bills—of doing the old four-legged frolic with his wife."

Will stared at his brother. To publicly name a lady as having been free with her favors was considered terribly poor form among that class of gentleman. To name one's own wife was appalling.

"What did Munro do?" Will asked.

"Denied it, naturally. Wallace called him a liar, said he'd make him pay for humiliating him that way. He actually took a swing at Phil, but he was so soused that he ended up toppling into the next table. Larry and Ezra dragged him out of there and took him up to his room to sleep it off. I hear he woke up the next morning covered in his own sick."

Will shook his head.

"Meanwhile, that very same night," Harry continued with a grin as he raised his cigarette to his lips, "who do you suppose was lying in wait for Phil back home, but the wayward wife herself."

"Sophie Wallace?"

"The four of us went back there after dinner for cognac and cigars before heading out to Fat Zack's. You know, that little gaming hell over on—"

"I know it," Will said.

"Phil led the way up the service stairs," Harry said, "so he was the first to find her waiting there in his office. He told the rest of us to go ahead to Zack's and that he'd meet up with us later, but I confess my curiosity got the better of me. I lingered a while on the fourth-floor landing after the other two had left."

Will sighed and kneaded the back of his neck.

"She got right to the point." Harry picked a fleck of tobacco off his tongue and flicked it in Nell's direction. "Said she'd be free to marry now that Wallace was divorcing her, that she'd waited twenty years to be Phil's wife, and now was their chance, and so on and so forth. Phil told her she was too late, that he had plans to marry Becky Bassett. She became quite worked up at that—apparently she'd no idea it had gone that far. She implored him to reconsider, got down on her knees, literally."

"You could see them?" Will asked.

Harry nodded. "I'd crept up to the door. She begged and pleaded and declared her undying love. That might have actually generated a bit of pity on Phil's part, I thought, but then she made a fatal error. She told him he was all she had left in the world, that Wallace was threatening to take the house and leave her without a settlement, because of the adultery. She said she was no good at being alone, that she was too old for it, that Phil owed it to her, after all those years on her back, to make an honest woman of her at last. She should have known better than to take such a tack with a man like Phil Munro—telling him what he owed, what was expected of him. He yanked her to her feet and told her, in so many words, that men in his position didn't wed aging, round-heeled divorcees."

Nell winced.

"Lovely fellow, your friend Phil," Will said.

"She went completely round the bend." Harry grinned and shook his head. "Came after him with claws bared, shrieking like a wildcat. 'You heartless bastard. I gave you everything. You should roast in hell . . . ' All that sort of claptrap. He threw her down on the chaise and pulled her skirts up, with her fighting and screaming all the while. Told her he'd give her one last pop just to calm her down and help her get hold of herself, but then that would be the end of them."

Will said, "Please tell me you didn't stand there and watch."

Harry waved a dismissive hand. "Phil wouldn't have minded. It was rather exciting at first, with her thrashing and screaming. I was sure someone would come upstairs to see what the ruckus was, but nobody did."

What was it Catherine had said? *If it came to my attention that Philip was entertaining one of his female acquaintances, I merely ignored the fact and went on about my business.*

"After a minute or two," Harry said, "she gave up struggling and just sort of went limp—and then came the tears. Phil didn't seem to mind, just kept on giving it to her, but that's when I left for Zack's." He flung his cigarette butt to the ground and crushed it with his heel. "There's nothing like a weeping woman to ruin a bit of harmless fun. It's like a bucket of cold water every time."

"Harry," Will said on a long, weary sigh, "there are times when I wonder how you can bear being you."

Chapter 8

"UNCLE Will!" Gracie exclaimed when she opened the lid of the big, iron-banded trunk she'd just unwrapped. "Oh, thank you! Thank you!" Her little friends, gathered around her like a bouquet of spring flowers in their frocks of taffeta and satin, contributed a chorus of oohs and ahhs.

The velvet-lined trunk, which bore the label M. JUMEAU—PARIS, housed six exquisite bisque fashion dolls, each wearing a traditional provincial costume. "They represent different regions in France," Will explained as the dolls were passed from one enraptured little girl to the next. "That one with the lace bonnet and the blue neckerchief is from Poitou. The one you're holding, Gracie, with the blue skirt, is from Brittany. The others are from Provence, Alsace, Pyrenees, and Bourgogne."

The trunk yielded up a vast collection of accessories, as well—hats, fans, shoes, stockings, gloves, brushes, combs, jewelry, baskets, purses, mirrors, even pets, one for each doll; two dogs, two cats, a duck, and a lamb.

"Look!" said one of the girls as she turned the head of the Burgundian doll to the side. "It moves!"

This innovation inspired a new flurry of excitement. The girlish squeals put Nell in mind of a skyful of bats. Nurse Parrish awoke with a start from her armchair doze in the corner, looked around blearily, and went back to sleep.

"They're wonderful! Oh, Uncle Will, I love them. I love *you*." Gracie opened her arms to Will, who knelt to return the embrace.

"I love you, too, *ma petite*." Will kissed his daughter's cheek and pulled her close, burying his face in her hair.

Nell felt a fist close around her heart, squeezing, squeezing . . . She noticed Viola, watching Will and Gracie from her Merlin chair in the doorway of the festively decorated front parlor. The older woman looked up and met Nell's gaze. Even from across the room, Nell could see her eyes glimmering wetly in the sunlight sweeping in through the windows.

Viola reached into her sleeve for her handkerchief, but Max Thurston, standing behind her with his hands on the grips of her chair, swiftly produced his own and shook it out for her. The elderly playwright had met the Hewitt matriarch only about an hour ago, when he arrived for Gracie's birthday tea with a picnic hamper containing a beribboned poodle pup for Gracie and a flagon of Martinez cocktails for himself, but they seemed to have taken to each other with remarkable speed. Not that surprising, really, when

Nell thought about it. Max and Viola were both iconoclasts in their own way, both outsiders stuck, for better or for worse, in the gilded cage of Boston aristocracy.

Max bent to Viola and whispered something. Nell read his lips: "Are you quite all right, my dear?" Only Max could get away with calling a lady he'd just met—one of the most venerable matrons in Boston, no less—"my dear."

Viola returned her gaze to her son and granddaughter for a long moment, then nodded to Max and said something Nell couldn't make out. He backed her chair out of the doorway and wheeled her down the hall.

Nell felt a hand on her arm and turned to find Will standing next to her. "Meet me in the garden?" he asked.

"I've got to help serve the cake and mulled wine," she said, "and then I'll be out."

SHE found him stretched out in the afternoon sun on the little stone bench that was the focal point of Viola's frowsily charming back garden. Dressed as he was, in a fine black frock coat, eyes closed, fingers laced on his stomach, he might have resembled a corpse laid out for viewing were it not for his healthy color. He'd been pallid when she first met him, and thinner, his eyes cast in shadow beneath that deep brow, a rapacious thrust to his jaw. Those sharp-carved features looked not so much predatory nowadays as patrician. Will Hewitt had the kind of face one saw on ancient Roman coins.

"Mulled wine for five-year-olds?" he murmured with his eyes still closed.

"It's more sugar water than anything else," Nell said as

she strolled toward him. "There's just a pint of port in that entire punchbowl."

Opening his eyes, he said, "Just enough booze to make the wee misses feel chic and daring. The lure of sin starts young."

Swinging up to a sitting position, he patted the bench next to him. Nell sat, brushing the dust of the bench off the back of Will's coat. He smiled at her, and it struck her suddenly that this sort of offhand tidying was the type of thing a wife might do for a husband. She drew back, mildly embarrassed.

"No, please." Turning to face away from her, Will said over his shoulder, "I'd hate to walk about looking like a dustman and not know it."

She continued, all too aware, as she smoothed her hands over his shoulders and down his arms, of his lean, solid body through the velvety wool.

Their silence only made her more self-conscious, so she said, "I saw Eileen Tierney in church this morning. The Bassetts' maid?"

He nodded. "The girl with the clubfoot. Did you speak to her?"

"She spoke to *me*," Nell said, pulling his coat taut with one hand as she swept it off with the other. "She came up to me as I was waiting for confession before mass. She'd just made confession herself, and she asked Father Gannon what he thought about the idea of surgery to repair her clubfoot. He said God helps those who help themselves, and that he knew and trusted me, and if I thought it was a good idea, it probably was. There." She gave his back one final, awkwardly chummy swat. "Not a speck left."

He smiled at her again as he turned to face her. "It's a novel thing to be tended to. Quite pleasant, actually. Thank you."

It *would* be a novel thing, Nell realized, for a man who'd been spent most of his youth among uncaring relatives and schoolmasters, and his adult years fending for himself in the war, in Andersonville, and then in a long, smoky succession of gaming hells and opium dens.

"Your Father Gannon sounds like a good man," Will said.

"He is." It pleased Nell that the irreligious Will should make such an observation. "Eileen's only qualms at this point have to do with . . . Well, she's very young, and very innocent, and . . ."

"And she doesn't like the idea of strange men touching her," Will said.

"She doesn't even want to be alone in a room with a man, even a doctor. She made me promise to be there when she met with you."

"Did you set a date?"

"Tuesday morning at nine o'clock. I hope that's all right, because she gets half a day off on Tuesdays, so long as she's finished all her chores the night before, and nothing else all week. Well, except for a couple of hours on Sunday mornings, for mass."

"Tuesday at nine is fine. And perhaps you wouldn't mind accompanying me on a visit to Sophie Wallace tomorrow morning? There are a few things I'd like to ask her, as you can imagine, and your perspective, as always, would be invaluable."

With a little shrug, Nell said, "I've got nothing but time

on my hands this week, seeing as Gracie will be in New York."

"I'd like to return Mr. Bassett's papers to his daughters, as well," Will said.

"Did you get a chance to look them over yesterday?" she asked.

He nodded as he lifted his bad leg over the good. "I gave the letters a fairly thorough read. As you know, Munro advised Bassett to buy gold over the summer, even if he had to take out a loan to do it. Bassett didn't want to go into debt. He'd never owed money, and he didn't want to start. He wanted to cash in his life insurance, but Munro told him he couldn't, because the payments had lapsed. So that's why, on Munro's advice but much against his better judgment, he ended up borrowing fifty thousand against the house and signing the letter of attorney."

"The life insurance had lapsed?" Nell asked. "It's worthless?"

With a grin, Will said, "Not being quite as prone to galloping assumptions as a certain little Irish governess I could name, I decided to look up an old acquaintance of mine, a surgeon named Bill Morland. He used to edit the *Boston Medical and Surgical Journal* back before the war, and he wrote quite an excellent book on diseases of the urinary organs. Now, as it happens, he's the chief medical examiner for New England Mutual. I paid a call on him yesterday and offered to buy him supper at Tuttle's in exchange for a bit of brain-picking on the subject of life insurance."

"And?"

"And it seems the Commonwealth of Massachusetts

passed a law eight years ago to the effect that when some-one stops paying his premiums, the policy simply converts to term for a fixed number of years."

"Converts to term?" Nell said. "I'm afraid you've reached the limit of what I know about life insurance."

"Simply put, your beneficiaries can still collect the death benefit if you die—up until the end of the term—but you can't cash in the policy or do anything else with it. I showed Bill the five policies Bassett held, and he told me the first one was due to expire two months from now, in November, and the rest before the end of the year."

"So, Becky and Miriam *will* get the insurance money, but if their father had died just a few months later . . ."

Will raised his hands, palms up.

"Do they get it all," she asked, "or will some of it have to go to the Tenth National Bank to pay off Bassett's fifty-thousand-dollar loan?"

"I asked Bill that, too. He said there's some other law that makes the proceeds exempt from the claims of credi-tors."

"How fortunate for Becky and Miriam. Do you suppose they've known about this windfall that's awaiting them?"

"More to the point, have they known they wouldn't get a cent if Papa survived into next year? That might be worth finding out, I think. I also wouldn't mind getting my hands on a copy of the *Canterbury Tales* and figuring out this business about Dame Prudence's proverb."

"Dame Prudence from the *Tale of Melibee*?" Max Thurston emerged through the back door with a rosy Mar-tinez cocktail in a brandy snifter. He cut a striking figure, despite his advanced years, with his neatly trimmed goatee and dapper attire. Like most of Boston's elite, he affected a high-toned British accent, although his was perhaps more pronounced than most.

"Are you familiar with the *Tale of Melibee*?" Will rose from the bench, gesturing for Max to sit there.

"God help me," Max said as he limped into the garden with the aid of his antler-handled cane, "I had to memorize the blasted thing back at Andover—or parts of it. Loathed Chaucer for years after that." Lowering himself stiffly onto the bench, he said, "I got over it."

Will said, "Do you recall anything about a prov—"

" 'The goodnesse that thou mayst do this day, do it, and abide nat ne delaye it nat til tomorwe.' " Max raised his glass as if for a toast, and took a sip.

"Of course," Nell said as it came back to her. "I should have remembered that. What it amounts to is, never put off till tomorrow what you can do today."

Will said, "So the gist of the telegram was something like, 'The best laid schemes often go awry. Don't put off till tomorrow what you can do today. Forewarned is forearmed.' "

"Or even more simply put," Nell said, " 'Our plan is collapsing. Don't wait until tomorrow . . .' "

" 'Sell the gold immediately,' " Will finished. "Munro was forewarned, all right."

"He was in cahoots with the conspiracy," Nell said.

"*Phil* Munro?" Max said. "Can't say I'm surprised."

Will said, "He received a telegram warning him that Grant was about to sell federal gold in order to lower the price."

"Whereupon," Nell said, "he was able to sell his own gold—at a huge profit, of course—before it lost its value."

"That telegram had to be from someone very high up," Will said, "someone who knew every step the president was taking before he took it."

"Phil Munro had no lack of friends in high places," Max said as he raised his glass to his lips.

"Did you know him?" Nell asked.

Max sighed; the spark winked out in his eyes. "Virginia did." He meant his dear friend and confidante Virginia Kimball, who was found shot to death in her Beacon Hill townhouse the previous spring. A retired actress with a "reputation," Mrs. Kimball was notorious for her liaisons with wealthy and powerful men.

"Munro was one of her . . . gentleman friends?" Nell asked.

"For a few weeks last year. He treated her like a two-dollar . . ." Max glanced at Nell, then away, scowling. "For a while there, he even had her feeling like that about herself, the knave. I must admit, when I read in the paper that he'd killed himself, I thought, 'Well done, old chap.' My only regret was that he hadn't done it before he took up with Virginia."

"It wasn't suicide," Will said. "I'm fairly well convinced, after performing the postmortem and examining the location of his death, that he was murdered."

"How very unsurprising." Max raised his glass again. "Here's hoping it was painful."

"He was a rotter, no doubt about it," Will said. "He'd bought gold for a number of men, which he dumped along with his own when he got the warning to sell— except for one fellow, whom he appears to have set out to ruin."

"That sounds like Phil Munro, all right." Max shook his head in evident disgust. "As for who might have sent the warning, he used to brag ad nauseam to Virginia about his contacts in Washington and New York—politicians, railroad men, financiers . . . She wrote down the names in her Red Book, which I have, of course. I reread it at night when I can't sleep. Jay Gould was one of Munro's cronies. And Commodore Vanderbilt. There was a senator, some congressmen, some judges . . . I don't recall all the names. I can look them up if you'd like. Oh, there was that speculator who married President Grant's sister a couple of months ago . . ."

"Abel Corbin?" Will said. "He was in the Gold Ring, but the initials on the telegram were G.B."

"G.B. . . ." Max swirled the ruby liquid in his glass, watching the cherry spin round and round. Suddenly he stopped. "George Boutwell." He looked at Will, then at Nell. "George Boutwell, the Sec—"

"Secretary of the Treasury," said Nell, who'd read his name in the paper just that morning. "That's pretty high up."

"And right in the eye of the storm," Will said. "When Grant decided to sell those four million in gold, it was Boutwell who made it happen."

"After warning Munro?" Nell said. "Is that possible?"

"I'd say it's probable," Will said. "According to the *Daily Advertiser,* Grant gave Boutwell the order to sell that gold at eleven o'clock, but it was past noon by the time the assistant treasurer in New York received his telegram to that effect. In the meantime, Boutwell had time to warn not just Munro, but possibly others. It would have all been arranged in advance. Remember what Munro's sister said about his always having an escape plan? I think Secretary Boutwell was his escape plan."

Max said, "Boutwell was just a congressman last year, when Munro was boasting about him to Virginia, but he was managing Johnson's impeachment, so that made him a fairly big bug. Munro told Virginia that Boutwell had been a sort of mentor to him when he was growing up in Brookline. He and Munro's father both taught public school there, before Boutwell entered politics. He took Munro under his wing, got him a scholarship to Harvard, and helped him out in business afterward."

"It would seem he's still helping him out," Nell said.

An aria of canine squeaks drew their attention to the back door, through which raced Gracie's new poodle pup, a reddish-brown fluff-ball dwarfed by the half-undone blue bow around his neck. He spied them and attempted a detour toward the carriage house, but Will leaned down and scooped him up in one large hand.

"Making a break for it, are you?" he asked as he raised the puppy to his face. "Too many young ladies trying to hold and pet you? A handsome young lad such as yourself must get used to such attentions."

"Clancy!" called Gracie as she ran out of the house. "Uncle Will, have you seen . . ." She yelped with delight when Will held the puppy out to her. "Clancy, you naughty boy," she scolded as she took him, rubbing his softly crimped fur against her cheek. "You oughtn't to wun away."

"Giving you a bit of trouble, is he?" Max asked

the child. "I'll be more than happy to take him back if you—"

"*No!*" Gracie spun away, cradling the animal to her chest. "I love him. And Nana says I can take him on the twain and the ship tomowwow." It was clearly the journey, not the destination, that had captured the child's fancy. To Will, she said, "I get to take the dolls, too—the whole twunk. But I have to be careful not to lose any of the little parts."

"Rubbish," Will said as he tweaked one of her curls. "Being careful negates the whole purpose of play. If you lose anything, I'll order a replacement."

Gracie leaned against him, saying, "I wish you could come with me. And Miseeney, and Mr. Thurston. All of you."

Nell said, "I wish I could come, too, buttercup. I'll miss you." She would, too, having never been separated from Gracie once in the five years she'd been caring for her.

Gracie came over to Nell and placed Clancy on her lap, where he sank happily into her pillowing silk skirts. Laying her own head next to the puppy, the child said, "Miseeny, when you and Uncle Will get mawwied, can I come live with you?"

Nell and Will looked at each other. Neither of them had ever mentioned their bogus courtship to her, nor, of course, had Viola, but servants tended to chatter rather freely in the presence of children. Max was regarding them curiously over the rim of his glass, as if they were actors in a play he'd come to watch.

Nell found her tongue first. "Don't you like living with Nana?" she asked as she stroked both Gracie's hair and Clancy's downy fur.

"I won't if you're not here. Nurse Pawwish sleeps all the time, and she doesn't play with me, and she smells like old, wotten woses." Nell couldn't argue with that, Edna Parrish having always been rather excessively fond of rosewater.

"Sometimes I pwetend you and Uncle Will are my mama and papa," Gracie said.

Nell didn't look up to meet Will's gaze, although she saw him looking at her. In a way, the three of them *were* like a little family. Gracie was Will's daughter, after all, and Nell was rearing her. They could never be a family for real, of course, but how could one explain the reasons for that to a child of five? *You see, Gracie, I'm secretly married to a convicted felon, although Nana doesn't know it, and I can't divorce and remarry, or my church will kick me out. So Uncle Will and I aren't really engaged, but we're making believe so people won't think I'm his mistress . . .*

"Excuse me." Mrs. Mott, the Hewitts' housekeeper, had materialized in the door to the house. "Mrs. Hewitt requires the child in the parlor."

Gracie looked up at Nell with an eloquently baleful expression. There was no love lost between her and the frostily severe Mrs. Mott.

"Go on, now." Nell patted the child's cheek. "Mustn't keep Nana waiting."

Leaning over the curled-up puppy, Gracie whispered, "I think he's asleep."

Nell said, "You can leave him with me for now. Run along."

Will reached into his coat as he watched his daughter disappear into the house. His hand remained there for a moment, on his tin of Bull Durhams, no doubt, before he withdrew it, empty.

"You should tell her the truth," Max said.

Nell and Will both turned to look at him.

"Do you think I'm blind?" Max asked with a knowing little smile. "She's got your eyes," he told Will, "your hair, your height . . . And why else would a lady like your delightful mother, who's already done her bit by raising four sons to adulthood, have adopted a chambermaid's baby? If *I* can sort it out, doddering old dowager that I am, others will do so soon enough. Eventually, Gracie herself will find out—probably through some vicious playmate's taunt. Wouldn't it be better to tell her now, yourself, when it will bring her joy rather than anguish?"

"It's . . . not that simple," Will said.

"It couldn't be simpler," Max countered. "She already looks to you as father figure. Once you marry Nell, you can bring her up as your own, and all will be right with the world."

Max's certitude seemed to fade as he watched Nell and Will exchange a look.

"You *are* still engaged, aren't you?" he asked. "I mean, I know it's never been official, but everyone knows."

Will glanced at Max, then back at Nell, lifting his shoulders, as if to say, *Why not tell him?*

He was right. Max was a good friend, and one they could trust with a confidence. Turning to Max, she said, "People know what we've let them think."

Max looked at her, then at Will. He swallowed down his Martinez, set the empty glass on the bench beside him, and sat back with his arms folded, awaiting the explanation.

Nell said, "Rumors were starting. It was either concoct a sham courtship or stop spending time together entirely—which, among other things, would make it very difficult for Will to see Gracie."

"What a marvelous premise for a comedic farce," Max said. "I must remember to write it down when I get home."

He didn't know the half of it, but he'd been enlightened quite enough for one day, Nell thought. Her past, should it become known, had the potential to destroy her.

"As for telling Gracie the truth about me," Will said, "it would only confuse and distress her. Other children have fathers who live with them, who conduct normal family lives, who are always there. I'm a professional gambler, Max, and a nomadic one."

"Not anymore."

"I'm just teaching as a favor to Isaac. When this term is over . . ." Will glanced at Nell, then away. "I'm not the kind of steady, reliable fellow Gracie deserves to have as a father."

"Yes, well, you're the only one she's got," Max said, "and she absolutely adores you."

Grimly Will said, "She feels that way now, because she's too young to see me for what I truly am. When she's older and more perceptive, even if she comes to suspect the truth, she'll be grateful that I never openly acknowledged her."

Bracing both hands on the cane, Max hauled himself to his feet with a disgusted grunt and hobbled up to Will. "Bollocks." Turning toward Nell, he executed an arthritically dignified bow. "A thousand apologies, my dear, but it had to be said."

"I quite understand."

Max went back into the house, shaking his head.

Will started reaching into his coat, made a fist, and rubbed the back of his neck, his gaze on the brick garden walk. "Do *you* think I should tell her?"

Nell thought about it for a moment as she ran her fingers through the sleeping puppy's fur. "I think you should discuss it with your mother, and if she thinks—"

"What do *you* think?" he demanded, pinning her with that darkly intent gaze.

Forcing herself to meet his eyes unwaveringly, she said, "I've told you before, Will, you're a better man than you think. Gracie knows it. That's why she loves you. Yes, you should tell her."

"What am I to say when she asks if she can live with us after we're married?"

That one was tougher. "Perhaps . . . that it's to be a long engagement, several years. Then, when she's older and can understand, you can tell her the truth."

"What truth? Which parts of it?"

"Well, not about Duncan, of course, but that . . . that we're not really . . . that we can't . . . that it's not like that between us." Holding his gaze, she said quietly, "That it can't be that way between us."

He looked away, his jaw tight. The puppy made an odd little cooing sound, yawned, and settled back into his silken nest with a somnolent little grunt.

Will said, "I'm going to Shanghai when the term is over."

She gaped at him. *Shanghai.* It had been one of his old haunts, notorious as a hotbed not just of gambling, but of every other sin imaginable.

Finally, she said, "Why?"

He stuck his hands in his trouser pockets and shrugged with a nonchalance that looked forced. "It's what I do."

"How long will you be gone?"

Frowning at the ground, he said, "It's hard to say. The trip itself is much shorter than it was before the railroads merged. I'll take the train to San Francisco and a steamer from there."

"But how long . . . how long do you think you'll be in Shanghai?"

He shrugged. "I might travel down the coast to Hong Kong. If I do, I'll probably spend a while in Hangchow—I have friends there. And I wouldn't mind seeing Tibet again. Of course, that's a fairly grueling overland journey."

"Six months?" she asked. "A year?"

He just shook his head, still not looking at her.

Are you ever coming back? Not wanting to ask it, because she wasn't sure she wanted to hear the answer, Nell looked down and stroked the puppy, just to have an excuse not to look at him. Whether he was gone half a year, a year, or God forbid, forever, she knew she would never stop missing him . . . wondering what kind of trouble he was getting into, if he was slipping back into his old ways . . .

He liked teaching, loved the research; he'd all but told her as much. Isaac Foster said he was brilliant at it, that it seemed like a perfect fit for him.

He came to sit beside her. For a while, neither of them spoke.

"You seem displeased," he said.

She drew in a calming breath, let it out. "I want what's best for you, Will, and I don't think it's best for you to go halfway 'round the world to play cards and . . ." She shook her head.

He said, "It's been a year since I've tasted opium."

"I know that. I'm not really worried about that."

"Not at all?"

"Not much. I just don't see the point to going so far away. There are gaming hells aplenty right here in Boston, if that's what you want. And you'd still have . . ." *Me.* "Gracie. And and the medical school . . . Isaac, Max . . ."

He smiled. "I'd be lying if I said I wasn't a little torn about the trip myself. Traveling like that . . . it's a wretched life, really."

"Then why do it?"

"Because being here . . ." He glanced at her, sighed. "In some ways, it's even more wretched."

As she was trying to compose a response to that, he said, "If you really think it would be best for me to stay, I could probably be persuaded."

"How?" she asked. "Reason doesn't seem to work."

"A kiss might."

She stared at him. The afternoon sun ignited his eyes, giving them a strangely golden radiance.

"Just one," he said softly. "I won't ask for a second. Ever. I promise. And I'll remain in Boston, and we can go on as before."

Her face was as hot as a pan of coals, but he didn't tease her about it, as he normally would. He just looked at her, very quietly, waiting for her answer.

"I don't . . ." She looked away and cleared her throat. "I don't think that would be very wise."

"Wisdom is overrated."

"I'm a married woman, Will."

"Are you honestly trying to tell me you owe fidelity to a man who once nearly killed you? You should have divorced him years ago."

"My fidelity isn't to Duncan, it's to the Church. If I were to divorce him and remarry, I'd be excommunicated."

"From the Catholic Church." Will closed a hand around her arm, leaning in close. "Not from God."

This was the first time she'd heard him speak of God as more than an abstract, somewhat archaic concept.

"The Church . . ." she began. "You don't understand. When I was at my lowest point, it helped me to remake myself into the person I wanted to be. It's been my bulwark."

"It's been your crutch, Nell. Perhaps it's time to set it aside."

"You want me to turn my back on my faith?"

"I want what's best for you, and what's best is to divorce Duncan. Then, if you ever choose to remarry, and you *are* excommunicated, it will be the *Church* turning its back on you, not God." In a low, earnest voice, Will said, "God would never forsake you. You must know that."

Nell was stunned into silence not just by the content of this speech—Will Hewitt sounding almost like a believer— but by the passion with which he'd delivered it.

Looking down at his hand on her arm, he apparently realized how tightly he was gripping her, and released his hold. He stood, dragged his hands through his hair, and said, "I've distressed you. I didn't mean to. I apologize."

Will walked down the path to the house, pausing in the doorway with one hand on the jamb. He stood there with his back to her for a moment, then turned, and with a somber little smile, said, "You're probably right about this kiss. I'm a selfish cur, or I never would have asked. Please forget I did."

Chapter 9

"MISS Sweeney and Dr. Hewitt to see Mrs. Wallace," said Will as he handed his card to the young parlor maid who answered their knock at Sophie Wallace's Pemberton Square townhouse the following morning. The maid invited them to wait in the imposing, marble-and-mahogany front hall while she went toward the back of the house to fetch her mistress.

She retreated down a long, dimly lit corridor toward a man whom Nell took to be the butler, clean-shaven as he was, and dressed all in black, save for a gray silk cravat. As the maid was about to pass him, he halted her with a soft-spoken, "One moment, Colleen." He took the card from her, withdrew a pair of spectacles from inside his coat, and read it.

Looking up, he removed the spectacles and regarded

Nell and Will curiously for a moment, then strode toward them, Colleen close on his heels. "I say, have we met? I'm Frederick Wallace."

F. Wallace—3:30

He moved out and initiated divorce proceedings... made quite an ass of himself in the dining room of the Parker House night before last...

Freddie Wallace was middle-aged and of average build, with smallish eyes, a candlewax pallor, and wetly oiled hair somewhere in that dreary borderland between brown and gray. He had a slightly nasal voice pitched high, making him seem younger than his appearance would suggest.

Extending his hand, Will said, "I don't believe we've had the pleasure. William Hewitt." With a nod toward Nell, he said, "And this is Miss Cornelia Sweeney. We're looking into the circumstances surrounding the death of your late client, Mr. Philip Munro."

Wallace's eyebrows quirked, almost imperceptibly; otherwise his bland expression remained unchanged. "Terrible thing. Ghastly. He, er . . . I was under the impression Munro . . . put an end to himself."

Choosing his words with obvious care, Will said, "The matter must be investigated before a final determination can be made. As I was the surgeon who performed the postmortem on Mr. Munro, it falls to me to make the necessary inquiries."

Wallace nodded slowly, his eyes, like beads of blue glass, trained on Will. "And your purpose in calling on my wife?"

Will hesitated, clearly at a loss as to how to answer that. *We understand she'd been banging the deceased* would be a bit indelicate.

Leaping in with the first thing that came to her, Nell said, "Actually, Mr. Wallace, it was you we'd wanted to speak to, but, well, it was our understanding that you no longer reside here. We came here in hopes of learning your current address."

Will graced her with a near smile that meant she'd impressed him, then turned to Wallace with an expectant expression—as did the parlor maid, who'd been following the conversation with poorly concealed interest.

"Ah." Wallace's head bobbed slightly, as if he were a marionette whose puppet master had just a touch of palsy. "I, er, yes. I . . . well . . . I reside here now. Again. That is, I was away for a couple of weeks. Business, you know. But I'm back, so . . ." He twitched his shoulders, his lips pressed into a thin smile. "You need look no further."

"Excellent," Will said. "Then if you could indulge us for a few—"

"Unfortunately," said Wallace as he lifted a black bowler and a walking stick from a console table next to the door, "as I have an eleven o'clock meeting at the State House, this interview will have to take place at some more convenient time. If you'd care to make an appointment with my secretary"—he produced a card and handed it to Will—"I suspect I can accommodate you before the end of the week."

"I'm afraid our inquiries can't wait that long," Will said. "If you could spare a few minutes right now—"

"Punctuality is a virtue that I have cultivated with some effort over the years, Dr. Hewitt. I'm sorry, but—"

"Are you always punctual?" Nell asked.

Wallace looked affronted, or perhaps merely surprised, by the question. "Yes. As a matter of fact, I am."

"You were on time, then, for your three-thirty appointment with Philip Munro on Friday afternoon?"

Wallace looked down, plucked a pair of gray kid gloves out of the derby, and donned the hat, adjusting it just so. "That appointment, as you are no doubt aware, never occurred. By the time I arrived, Mr. Munro had already—"

"We know," Will said. "You were the one who found him on the front steps. According to his calendar, you were due at three-thirty, but his body was actually discovered ten minutes later, at three-forty."

Wallace tucked the walking stick under his arm and pulled on one of the gloves, scowling. "If I were prepared for this conversation, perhaps I could have the information you seek at my fingertips, so once again, I urge you to contact my secretary and—"

"If you *had* been on time," Will persisted, "I imagine you would have climbed the service stairs to Munro's office, where you would have found him waiting for you. You would have . . . done whatever it was you'd gone there to do, and left as you came, through the back door. But suppose you'd then returned to your buggy, which you would have parked, say, in an alley off the kitchen yard, and driven 'round to the front of the house—only to encounter Mr. Munro's body on the front steps at about three-forty."

"I'm not quite sure I know what your point is, Dr. Hewitt, and I'm not sure I want to." Pulling on the other glove rather jerkily, Wallace said, "It's a four-minute walk to the

State House. If I leave immediately, I might still be there on time. Miss Sweeney . . . Dr. Hewitt." He bowed curtly to Nell and Will, then turned toward the front door, which the maid scurried to open for him.

Will said, "Do you recall the incident Thursday night at the Parker House, Mr. Wallace?"

Wallace glared at him from the open doorway, clearly at a loss for words.

"I'm asking whether you recall," Will continued, "because, as I understand it—"

"I'd had a bit too much wine with dinner," Wallace said tightly. "As I'm unused to strong drink, it went to my head. Surely, Dr. Hewitt, there have been times in your own life that you would prefer not to be forced to relive."

"More than you can possibly imagine. I understand you accused Mr. Munro of . . . indiscretions with Mrs. Wallace."

Colleen's eyes widened as she held the door open; there would be no end of whispering and giggling in the servants' quarters tonight.

"I was inebriated," Wallace said. "And . . . laboring under a misapprehension. To say I regret the incident would be the height of understatement."

Nell said, "By 'misapprehension,' do you mean—"

"This conversation is over. Good day."

Nell and Will watched from the front stoop as Wallace half-walked, half-jogged south, toward Beacon Street and the State House. As soon as he was out of sight, they turned back and knocked on the front door.

Handing a second card to the befuddled Colleen, Will said, "Mrs. Wallace, if you please."

* * *

"WE'VE reconciled, Freddie and I." Sophie Wallace raised her demitasse to her mouth, pursing her lightly rouged lips to blow on it as she eyed Will over the rim of the diminutive cup. Reclining on a fainting couch in her drawing room, her morning dress of green silk gauze rippling onto the floor, pale ringlets framing a pretty if timeworn face, she put Nell in mind of Cleopatra on her barge.

Unlike her husband, Sophie had been perfectly willing to speak to them. It didn't hurt that Will had disingenuously asked her for "anything you might be able to tell us about your husband's client who passed away Friday afternoon. Mr. Wallace was in a hurry to make a meeting, so we thought perhaps you might indulge us?" It also didn't hurt, Nell knew, that Will was a tall, darkly handsome, seductively charming Englishman.

Nell and Will were shown to the drawing room, settled into deeply tufted chairs, and brought demitasse and lemon kisses. Their opening "small talk" had to do with their surprise at finding Mr. Wallace at home, having been told that he no longer lived there. Sophie had admitted their estrangement, but chalked it up to her husband's "quaint but rather flattering jealous streak."

"A gentleman can hardly look in my direction," she'd said, "without Freddie thinking he's got designs on me."

And now the news that she and Freddie had reconciled.

Nell said, "This reconciliation must be a source of great comfort to you, Mrs. Wallace."

Sophie merely sipped her coffee.

"Especially," Nell added, "in light of the circumstances."

Sophie fixed her gaze on Nell.

"That dreadful scene at the Parker House on Thursday night," Nell said, wondering if Sophie had been told of it. "I'd say half of Boston knows about your husband's jealous streak by now. Must have been terribly distressing for you."

Sophie drained her demitasse and refilled it. "I sent a note to Freddie the next morning, when I heard what he'd done, asking him to come here for lunch so that we could talk. I told him how distraught it had made me, knowing he'd bandied my name about like that in public—especially considering it wasn't even true."

"The . . . accusation, you mean?" Will asked. "About you and Philip Munro?"

"Freddie found a stickpin of Philip's in my boudoir a couple of weeks ago," Sophie said with a little roll of the eyes, "and jumped to the wrong conclusion. Stormed out of the house without giving me a chance to explain, and the next thing I knew, he'd moved out and sued me for divorce. I explained over lunch that I'd merely borrowed the pin from Philip so that I could have one like it made up for Freddie as a Christmas present. It's a very smart pin—I'd always admired it."

"I see," Nell said as she lifted her own dainty little cup and saucer. What she didn't see was why it should have taken two weeks for Sophie to share this all-important detail with her anguished husband.

"It was an emotional conversation," Sophie said. "I

couldn't contain my tears, and Freddie, poor dear, could never bear to see me weep. He was quite contrite about that scene at the Parker House, couldn't stop apologizing. I must admit, he wore me down. I forgave him, and we . . ." Her too-pink lips curved into a private little smile as her gaze flicked toward Will. "As I say, we reconciled."

Had Freddie actually believed his wife's tall tale about replicating the stickpin? Were her tears, however practiced, really that convincing? Or had he accepted her version of things merely in order to reunite with his beloved Sophie, while still knowing, in his heart, that she'd betrayed him with Philip Munro?

Sophie's own motives in all this seemed no less pathetic. Nell wanted to feel nothing but disdain for the aging coquette, with her ringlets and her sheer gown and her flirty eyes always sliding toward Will. She might have felt just that but for Sophie's final, degrading encounter with Phil Munro, as recounted by Harry—she begging him to marry her so that she wouldn't be alone, then weeping while he used her for the only thing he'd really ever cared about.

Sophie was telling Will that her husband had sent a footman to Munro's house during lunch, requesting an appointment at three-thirty that afternoon. "Freddie wanted to bury the hatchet—apologize to Philip for his little display at the Parker House, and hopefully convince him to keep him on as legal counsel. Philip has been a lucrative client for my husband, as you can imagine. It would have been devastating to lose him."

"Do you know whether Mr. Wallace was on time for that three-thirty meeting?" Will asked.

Sophie couldn't disguise a whiff of scorn when she said, "Freddie's always on time."

"The reason I asked," Will said, "is that Mr. Munro's body was found by your husband at three-*forty*. Either he was late arriving for his meeting, or he'd already been there for ten minutes or so before making the discovery."

Sophie thought about it for a moment as she reached for a lemon kiss. "I'm not really sure when Freddie left the house Friday afternoon, because I was gone by then. He was asleep when I left, and I didn't want to—"

Nell said, "Asleep?" as Will said, "You left?"

"He was, er, taking a little nap upstairs," Sophie said. "I had some shopping to do, and I didn't want to disturb him, so I just slipped out. I suppose I should have asked one of the maids to awaken him in time for his meeting with Philip, so if he *was* late, I suppose it's really my fault." She touched the little confection to her tongue before closing her mouth around it.

"That might explain the timing," Will said. "Do you recall when you returned home from shopping?"

Sophie looked thoughtful as the kiss dissolved in her mouth. "Four-thirty, perhaps? Freddie was already back home, and halfway through a decanter of whiskey. He just kept saying, 'He's dead . . . Phil is dead.' Poor thing, he was utterly beside himself. It was guilt—that's what I think."

"Guilt?" Nell said.

"Think about it. The last time he'd seen Philip was the night before, when he was drunk and screaming false accusations in a dining room full of people. And now that I think of it, if he'd only been on time for their meeting Friday afternoon, he might have been able to talk Philip out of jumping from that window."

"Mr. Munro didn't jump," Will said. "He was murdered, and his body thrown out of the window to make it look like suicide."

"Murdered," Sophie said quietly. "Are you sure?"

"We *would* like to be able to prove it," Nell said, thinking the time had come to, as Will would say, lay their cards on the table. "It would help if we could get an idea of his state of mind in the days preceding his death. Can you tell us how he appeared to you when you visited him in his office Thursday evening?"

Sophie stilled in the act of lifting her demitasse to her mouth. Her gaze shifted from Nell to Will. By the time it shifted back, her expression had grown hard and opaque. She lowered her cup without taking a sip, stood, and strode across the room toward a bell pull in the corner, her filmy gown billowing behind her. "Colleen will show you out."

Nell said, "Mrs. Wallace—"

"What you're implying is outrageous, and if you think I'm going to sit still and listen to—"

"There was a witness," Nell said.

Sophie froze with her hand around the bell pull.

"Someone was listening from the fourth-floor landing," Nell said. "And . . . watching."

Sophie closed her eyes, looking suddenly much older than she had before. She removed her hand from the cord and lowered herself into a little hard-backed corner chair. "What do you want?"

"Not to tell your husband, you mean?" Nell asked. "We have no reason to—"

"It's information we want," Will said, with a furtive little glance at Nell. "You could help us a great deal just by answering a few questions, and in return, you have my word that we'll keep these matters as confidential as we possibly can."

Sophie regarded them listlessly.

"How long had you and Mr. Munro been . . . intimately acquainted?" Will asked.

She drew in a breath and let it out slowly. "Twenty years, more or less."

"Did you love him?" Nell asked.

Sophie shrank into the chair, staring blankly at the carpet. "I was a fool."

"Did he love you?"

"The concept of love is foreign to him—*was* foreign to him."

Nell said, "I can't imagine how you must have felt Thursday night. I mean, the things he said . . . and did . . ."

"I was shocked," Sophie replied numbly, her gaze still on the floor. "Devastated. Enraged. I wanted to claw his face open, gouge out his eyes."

"Did you wish he was dead?" Nell asked.

Looking up, Sophie said, "Wouldn't you have?"

"You'd known him for twenty years," Will said. "Who, among his acquaintances, might have grown to loathe him, or felt threatened by him?"

"Who didn't?" Sophie asked with a sort of weary bitterness.

"Do you know anything about his relationship with the Bassett sisters?" Nell asked.

Sophie groaned. "The younger one was after his money.

God knows that's the only reason a Bassett would agree to marry a parvenu like Philip."

"Yes, but *you're* from one of the old Brahmin families," Nell said, "and my understanding is that you would have married him in a heartbeat."

"As I've already pointed out," Sophie said, "I am a fool. Becky Bassett, her idiot chatter notwithstanding, is actually rather shrewd. Certainly not the type to let messy emotions get in the way of an advantageous marriage. For all I know, she may have detested Philip. I'm fairly certain she was nothing more to him than a pretty young blonde with a good name. She'd get the money, he'd get the name. A match made in heaven's countinghouse."

"What about Miriam?" Will asked.

"Miriam." Sophie said it as she might have said, *Pig dung.* "Miriam Bassett is not entirely what she seems."

A popular refrain, that. "How do you mean?" Nell asked.

Sophie stood, smirking, and sauntered back to the fainting couch. "She likes to make herself out as the epitome of moral purity, but I assure you, it's all an act. I've known her since she was sixteen, and one thing she's not is pure."

"Did she know Mr. Munro then?" Will asked.

"Oh, yes," Sophie said as she settled back on the couch, spreading her skirts out prettily. "I met her through him. We'd been . . . involved, he and I, for a couple of years, but he was still at Harvard, so I didn't find it odd that he hadn't proposed to me yet. I assumed, once he'd graduated and was earning a decent living . . ." She looked away in evident disgust. "I assumed wrong. One day, after we'd been . . . well, suffice it to say he was feeling relaxed, a bit too much so, perhaps, he told me he'd decided to steal Miriam Bassett away from Chet Langdon."

"Chet . . . ?"

"Her beau. Excellent family, wonderful prospects . . ." Sophie waved a listless hand. "Everything that sort thinks is important. Chet was due to leave on his Grand Tour soon, so Philip planned to pounce while he was away."

"He told you this," Nell asked, "even though you and he were—"

"It was when I first realized he thought of me not so much as a lover, but as a sort of chum who was conveniently free with her favors. It was an eye-opener, and not a pleasant one."

"No, I don't imagine so."

"He rhapsodized at great length about Miriam's many assets—her breeding, her beauty, but most of all, her virtue. She was the perfect Brahmin bride for a high-reaching upstart such as he, and he was determined to wed her. He'd been wooing her with every romantic trick at his disposal, he told me, redoubling his efforts every time she rebuffed him. *Rebuffed* him! Here I was, dreaming about the day when he would finally get down on one knee before me, and this absurd little mouse was showing him the cold shoulder."

"So Munro thought she'd come 'round once this Chet fellow was safely overseas, eh?" Will said. "Out of sight and out of mind?"

"That was the idea, but he was in for a surprise." Sophie sat forward and lowered her voice, although they were the only people in the room. "Right after Chet left for Europe in June of eighteen-fifty, Miriam came to see me, which was rather unexpected. We knew each other, but we weren't exactly what you'd call friends. She was several years younger than I, and we had nothing in common."

"Except for Philip Munro," Nell said.

"Not for long." Sophie chose another lemon kiss from the plate and sat back, smiling. "It took Miriam forever to come to the point. She was shaking like a rabbit. She told me I was the only person she could think of to consult about a particular matter, because of my—how did she put it?—'familiarity of a certain nature with gentlemen.' "

"She knew about you and Munro?" Will asked.

"She knew about *me,* because I was never quite as discreet as I might have been back then. It wasn't widely known, at the time, that Philip and I were lovers, but everyone seemed to know that Sophie Cabot was no blushing maiden. Nevertheless, imagine my surprise when Miriam finally screwed up the courage to ask me how she could tell if she was in the family way." Sophie popped the little confection into her mouth, grinning like a cat.

Nell said, "She and Chet?"

Sophie smiled as she washed the kiss down with a sip of coffee. "Evidently, and now he was in Europe, and Miriam, in her pathetic naïveté, was trying to figure out if she was going to have to cable him home for a hasty wedding. She'd taken no precautions, of course—hadn't even known they existed."

"Was she with child?" Will asked.

"She was too mortified to discuss the particulars of her own situation," Sophie said. "Just wanted the basic information, which I gave her. She thanked me and left, whereupon

I promptly called on Philip and told him what any female in my position would—that his darling Miriam of the spotless reputation was, in fact, carrying Chet Langdon's baby."

"But you didn't know that for sure," Will said.

"Let us just say I assumed it from the nature of our conversation."

"You assumed what you wanted to assume," Nell said.

"Don't we all? It seemed to do the trick, in any event, because Philip abandoned the idea of courting her. In fact, whenever he spoke of her afterward, it was in the most deliciously scathing terms."

"I gather she wasn't actually pregnant," Nell said, "if she didn't end up marrying Chet."

"Actually, she left that fall for Miss Finch's in New York, which is where she spent the entire school year—or so we were told."

"You don't believe it?" Will asked.

"She may have done," Sophie said with a shrug. "Girls either finished up there, or at Payne's, here in Boston. I encouraged Philip to think she was off spawning Chet Langdon's bastard. When she came home in the spring of 'fifty-one, Chet wasn't in the picture anymore. I've no idea why it ended."

"Was she still active in your social circle?" Nell asked.

"No, she more or less turned her nose up at the rest of us after she came back from New York—kept to herself and dried up into a tiresome old maid."

Nell said, "We heard a rumor that she'd been pursuing Mr. Munro over the past few months—notwithstanding his engagement to Becky."

Sophie paused with the little cup halfway to her mouth. "Who told you that?"

"Someone in a position to know," Will said.

Lowering the cup, Sophie muttered, "I'll be damned."

"Does it seem credible to you?" Nell asked.

Sophie seemed to ponder that. "Philip had a way of making females lose perspective. And he was an insatiable swordsman. I knew about the other women, but I always knew I was the one he came back to." Setting the demitasse aside, she asked, with patently feigned indifference, "Was he sleeping with her?"

"Apparently not," Nell said. "What we were told—and it isn't necessarily the truth, or the entire truth—is that she was in love with him but resisting his physical advances—that she wanted to be his wife, not his mistress."

Sophie nodded. "That makes sense, knowing Miriam. I can't imagine she was very keen on the idea of Philip's marrying her sister."

"From all accounts, she found the prospect devastating."

"She must have been horribly jealous," Sophie mused. "Jealousy can drive people to rash acts, even violence. Have you considered the possibility—"

"We're considering all possibilities." Will stood, shaking out his frock coat. "Thank you for your cooperation, Mrs. Wallace. Miss Sweeney and I appreciate it greatly."

"For what it's worth," Sophie said as she rose off the fainting couch, "I'd be more than willing to testify in court as to Miriam's . . . deficits of character, the pregnancy worries and all that. Whatever it might take to secure a murder conviction."

Or to deflect suspicion from herself. Nell mused as

Sophie walked them to the front door—from herself, or from her husband.

"What did you buy Friday?" Nell asked as Sophie held the door open for them.

The other woman regarded her blankly.

"On your shopping trip, when your husband was napping." Nell gave Sophie what she hoped was a disarmingly friendly smile. "It's a marvelous time to be looking for hats and boots and such, because all the new autumn styles are in the shops. Did you get anything good?"

"Nothing at all, actually. You know how sometimes you want everything you see, and other times nothing strikes your fancy? This was one of those other times," she said, and closed the door.

Chapter 10

"**E**ILEEN!" called Becky Bassett for a second time, her voice muffled by the door with the peeling black paint. When at last she opened it, she greeted Nell and Will with a sheepish smile and an apology for making them wait. "The girl does the marketing on Monday afternoons. I always forget. I'll be calling her name till I'm hoarse in the throat, and Miriam will say, 'Becky, you little goose, don't you remember? It's Monday afternoon. She's not even here.' And I'll feel like an absolute ninny. But here I am, with my ghastly manners, letting you cool your heels on the front porch. Come in, come in! You're here to see Miriam, I suppose?"

"And you as well," said Will, who had the green folio tucked under his arm.

As they entered the front hall, Nell saw, through the

open doorway to the right, a coffin on a board balanced between two tall-backed chairs. Noah Bassett was laid out in the suit of clothes Dr. Tanner had chosen for him, his mouth in a sort of slack grimace that made him look very unlike the genial fellow he'd been in life. Pots of lavender were scattered about the room, sweetening the murky smell of death.

Becky had on the same frock she'd been wearing Saturday, augmented with a white muslin collar and the weeping cuffs she'd been sewing during their prior visit. She led them into a large, high-ceilinged dining room, where her sister and Dr. Tanner sat at a too-small table, nursing cups of tea. The floor was naked wooden planks, save for a crumb cloth under the table, and the furnishings sparse, making the space seem even more cavernous than it was. Yellowed oilcloth shades covered the windows, casting an amber patina over the room and its occupants. For a brief moment, as the black-clad couple turned their gazes toward the doorway, Nell was put in mind of one of those old, thickly varnished Flemish paintings of domestic life.

The minister stood and bowed to Nell, a sheaf of papers in his hand, and explained that they'd been going over his eulogy for tomorrow's funeral service. Nell complimented Miriam's mourning gown, a well-tailored black dress with jet buttons, and asked if it was the one she'd been dyeing during their last visit, although she knew it wasn't.

"I'm afraid I had to give that dress to the rag man," Miriam told her. "It didn't take the dye properly."

Will waited until everyone was seated, then lowered himself into the chair next to Nell's and placed the folio on the table. "We found this in an iron closet in Philip Munro's office, and we thought you'd like to have it. It contains documents relating to your late father."

Becky eyed Will and Nell nervously, as if afraid they'd tattle about her blurting out the connection between Noah Bassett and Munro.

"Thank you," Miriam said. "I, er . . . Philip advised my father from time to time on financial matters. I didn't think to mention it the other day because, well, we weren't really very well acquainted with him. It was just a business relationship, you know, not personal."

Bristling at the bald lie, Nell said, "We know he was engaged to Becky. I'd say that's fairly personal."

Tanner sighed and looked toward Miriam, who stared at Nell with a half-open mouth, her face pinkening in the golden half-light. Wheeling on her sister, she said, "Did you tell them about—"

"No!" Becky yelped in her childlike voice. "I didn't, I swear it."

"It was only a matter of time before it came out," Tanner told Miriam in a low, gentle voice. "Candor is always the best policy. Regardless of how you felt about the man—"

"I had no feelings of any kind toward Philip Munro," Miriam said tersely. "The simple fact is that he and my sister were *never* engaged."

"Well, not officially," Becky said, "but we—"

"Not at all, not in any way." Turning stiffly to Nell and Will, Miriam said, "My father would not permit an engagement, therefore no engagement existed. Our family's dealings with Philip were strictly limited to the counsel he gave Papa. I say again, it was purely a *business* relationship."

"And, it would seem, an ill-advised one," Will said. "On Munro's advice, your father borrowed fifty thousand dollars against this house in order to buy gold."

Becky sucked in a breath. Tanner closed his eyes and rubbed his forehead. Miriam's only reaction was to gaze glumly down at the table.

Nell said, "Your father turned to Mr. Munro out of desperation. But if he was in financial straits before gold fell, afterward . . . well, he was destroyed. Not only penniless, but crushed by debt he could never hope to repay."

"I . . . I've no doubt Philip felt he was acting in my father's best interest," Miriam said. "I assume he invested in gold on behalf of the other gentlemen he advised. Why, he was ruined himself—otherwise, why would he have taken his own life?"

"He didn't," Will said. "At least, we don't think he did, in part because he had no reason to. He sold everyone's gold late Friday morning, his own and that of his clients, at a colossal profit—with the lone exception of your father, even though he knew the market was about to collapse."

"He *knew*?" Tanner said. "How could he have known?"

"He couldn't have known," Miriam scoffed. "No one knew."

Nell said, "The Secretary of the Treasury, George Boutwell, was an old friend of Mr. Munro's. Secretary Boutwell sent him a coded telegram Friday morning, warning him that it was time to sell."

"He . . . he did it on purpose?" Becky asked. "Mr. Munro ruined Papa *on purpose*?"

Tanner slumped back in his chair, shaking his head. "My God, why would he have done such a thing?"

"To punish Papa for not letting us marry," Becky said, as if it were obvious.

Miriam said, "If it's true that he meant to . . . to hurt Papa, perhaps—"

"*Hurt* him?" Becky sprang from her chair, eyes wide with outrage. "He meant to *destroy* him. He did destroy him. Papa killed himself because of what that man did to him."

"If . . . if it's true," Miriam said, "perhaps it was guilt that drove him to take his own—"

"*Guilt?*" Becky said. "He was incapable of guilt. He was a monster. I'm glad he's dead."

"Becky," Tanner said softly.

Miriam said, "Honestly, Becky . . ."

"How can you defend him?" Becky shrilled. "*Why* are you defending him? You despised him."

"I didn't—"

"If you didn't, then why did you raise such a fuss when we asked Papa for his permission to marry? Why did you call him the things you called him? You're the reason Papa wouldn't let us get married, and now you're talking as if we should feel sorry for him."

"I'm just saying we might try to understand—"

"*Understand?* I *understand* that Papa's lying in there"—Becky stabbed a finger toward the parlor—"in a coffin because of Philip Munro. And you're sitting in here making excuses for him."

Miriam stood, quivering. "That's enough, Becky."

"You make me sick," Becky spat out. "I don't know who I hate more right now, you or him."

"Get hold of yourself." Miriam grabbed Becky's arm.

Becky hauled back with her free hand and cracked her sister across the face with stinging force. Miriam cried out, her head whipping to the side, as Tanner leapt from his chair. Becky gasped and backed away, as if stunned by what she'd done, then lifted her skirts and fled from the room. A moment later, the front door banged behind her.

"Let her go," Tanner said as Miriam started after her sister.

"But—"

"She needs to collect herself. And so do you." The minister lowered his fiancée into her chair and nudged her chin to the side to inspect her reddened cheek. "Can you move your jaw?"

"I'm not hurt, just . . ." To Nell and Will, she said, "Becky's not herself. Please don't judge her. It's grief that's done this to her."

Grief? Nell said, "You'll forgive me, Miss Bassett, but it's been my impression that Becky and your father weren't particularly close."

Tanner, standing behind Miriam with his hands on the back of her chair, said, "If that's true, it might even amplify her grief. It can be confusing and difficult, saying goodbye to someone with whom one should have enjoyed a strong familial bond, but didn't."

"Was there some kind of antagonism between them?" Nell asked.

"There wasn't much of anything between them," Miriam said. "My father just never . . . took to Becky. It wasn't her fault. She was a lovely child. It was just one of those things."

Tanner said, "I've often thought perhaps he blamed her for the illness that claimed Mrs. Bassett's life."

"What?" Miriam seemed not just taken aback, but bewildered by the notion.

"Was it not shortly after Becky's birth," Tanner asked, "that your mother became unwell? She wasted away for two or three years before she passed on, and that's a painful thing to watch a loved one endure. Perhaps your father felt that she'd been depleted by bearing a child at her age."

"Mamá was thirty-eight," Miriam said. "That's not so very old."

Old enough, Nell thought, especially given her history of difficult pregnancies.

"It affected you, too," Tanner told Miriam, "your mother declining when Becky was so young. Your father once told me he thought you would have been a happier person if you hadn't been forced to take on Becky's care and rearing when other girls your age were larking about and flirting and just being young. He said girls are supposed to be looking for husbands when they get out of finishing school, not playing nursemaid to little sisters and sick mothers. He admitted his melancholia only made matters worse for you. It troubled him that you never laughed, that you seemed to feel as if everything and everyone was your responsibility. He said it was high time someone took care of *you*." With a tentative little smile, Tanner added, "I told him I meant to remedy that situation."

Miriam glanced up at her fiancé, then looked down, coloring slightly.

"You'll pardon me for saying so," Will said, "but Becky's

low opinion of Mr. Munro . . . well, it just strikes me as odd, given that they were betrothed. On the one hand, she called him a monster. On the other, she was furious at being refused permission to marry him."

"That marriage was to have been her one great righteous act," Tanner said, "her way of proving that she wasn't just a spoiled little child, that she could be as practical and selfless as Miriam."

"She knew Philip didn't love her," Miriam said. "All she was to him was a comely young girl with a pristine reputation and one of the best names in Boston. And she certainly didn't love him. She thought him arrogant and debauched. But he was fabulously rich, and we were growing poorer by the minute. She considered him our salvation. All she had to do was to condemn herself to a loveless marriage for the rest of her life."

"A pretty girl like Becky . . ." Nell began. "I'm surprised she didn't have her choice of well-heeled suitors."

"Where would she have met them?" Miriam asked. "She didn't go to dinner parties or balls or the opera. We couldn't afford a decent pair of gloves, not to mention the gowns and all the rest of it. We sold the horse and buggy years ago, and started turning down invitations. After a while, they just stopped coming. Philip would never have met her if he hadn't come to the house for that first meeting with Papa about his finances. When he started paying his addresses to her, she considered it a godsend."

Tanner said, "He talked her into keeping the courtship a secret from her father until they were ready to announce the engagement, but that tactic worked against him. Noah felt as if he'd been deceived, and that was one of the reasons he was so opposed to the marriage—that, and Munro's reputation. And of course, Noah knew perfectly well why Becky had agreed to marry him. He told me it was an unacceptable sacrifice on her part. He wanted her to marry for love, as he had, and he knew she could never love Philip Munro."

"How did *you* feel about Munro?" Nell asked the minister.

"I barely knew him, and I'd be loath to pass judgment if I did. I will admit I thought it was a mistake for Becky to marry him, but I understand her desire to return the Bassett family to their former prosperity. *I* was certainly in no position to do it. My income has never been more than modest, and I've no family money."

"The reason I asked how you felt about Mr. Munro," Nell said, "is that your name appears in his desk calendar. You had an appointment to see him at twelve-thirty Friday afternoon."

Miriam turned to gape at Tanner, who stepped back from her chair, hands raised in a pacifying gesture.

"You went to *see* him?" she asked in a tone of utter incredulity.

"I didn't mention it to you," he said, "because I didn't want you to be any more troubled than you already—"

"Why on earth? Why would you . . ."

"I knew how it weighed on you, Munro's threat to do whatever it might take to force your father to bless the marriage. I thought if I could just go there and talk to him—"

"About *what*? What . . . what did you talk about?"

Clearly unsettled by her reaction, Tanner said, "Nothing at all, as it turned out. News of the gold crash had started to circulate by the time I got to his office, and he was too busy to meet with me. I told him I'd come back Monday at two." With a glance at his pocket watch, he said. "That's where I'd be right now if he were still alive. My plan had been to reason with him, man to man. I wanted him to understand the impact his dogged pursuit of Becky was having on the family, that it was just pride driving him on, and that he and Becky would both be more content married to other people."

"Content?" Miriam said with an acerbic little laugh. "It was never about contentment, don't you understand that? It was about money. It was about status."

"You don't think I realize that?" Crouching down so that he could look her in the eye, Tanner said quietly, "You must not know me very well at all, Miss Bassett, to think me so obtuse. It's my fault. I've always been a bit too self-contained, too much a slave to propriety, always letting the mind lead the heart instead of the other way 'round. But believe me when I say that I see, and know, much more than may be evident upon casual observation."

"What do you know?" she asked unsteadily.

"I know you're filled with fear. And I know I'd do anything to take that fear away."

"If you're worried about losing the house, you needn't be." Will slid the life insurance policies out of the folio and handed them to her. "These are worth a hundred thousand dollars."

"So that's where they were," Tanner said as he returned to his seat.

"You knew about them?" Nell asked.

Tanner nodded. "Miss Bassett asked me to keep an eye

out for them when I was sorting through Noah's desk the other day."

"I'm surprised you were aware of the insurance," Nell told Miriam, "given your father's reluctance to discuss financial matters with you."

"I . . . found out recently," Miriam said.

"From your father?" Nell asked.

Miriam hesitated. "Yes."

Will said, "Becky knew, too?"

"I told her when I found out."

"The policies were due to expire within the next few months," Nell said. "How fortunate for you and Becky that they're still in force."

"I don't feel fortunate," Miriam said grimly. "Except, perhaps, that Becky didn't go ahead and marry Philip Munro, thinking we needed his money when we really didn't."

Now for the dicey bit. In discussing their strategy for questioning the evasive Miriam, Will had advocated for a confrontational approach. The more blunt and unexpected the questions, he'd said, the less prepared she'd be with her slippery prevarications.

"What a curious thing," Nell told her, "for a gentleman to have marital designs on two sisters, twenty years apart."

Miriam seemed dumbstruck. Tanner turned to stare at her. Clearly, this was news to him.

"Were we misinformed?" Nell asked. "We understood Mr. Munro pursued you rather avidly when you were young."

"Did he?" Tanner asked.

Miriam fanned out the insurance policies, then arranged them in a neat little stack. "He . . . made overtures, but I had no interest in them."

Tanner was studying her with quiet gravity.

Looking up, Miriam said, "Who, um . . . who told you about . . ."

"Mrs. Wallace," Nell said. "Mrs. Sophie Wallace. She would have been Miss Sophie Cabot when you—"

"I know who you mean," Miriam said.

"She was most forthcoming with information," Nell said carefully. "Most forthcoming. She told us about a very interesting conversation you and she had when you were sixteen. If you don't mind, I'd like to pursue that topic in greater depth."

"This isn't really the best time." Miriam cast a significant, if fleeting, glance at John Tanner.

"I realize that," Nell said, "and I apologize for the inconvenience, but the subject must be addressed."

On a capitulatory sigh, Miriam said, "Very well, but I . . . I can't stop fretting about Becky. Dr. Tanner, I wonder if you would be so kind as to go look for her. She probably headed west, toward the river. She likes to take walks there sometimes."

Tanner contemplated Miriam in silence for a moment; she wouldn't meet his eyes. He opened his mouth to say something, seemed to reconsider, then just stood, excused himself, and left.

Miriam shut her eyes when the door closed behind him, and sat back bonelessly in her chair.

Not knowing how long it would take Tanner to locate

Becky, Nell came right to the point. "There is some senti-ment among those close to Mr. Munro that you may have been involved in his death."

"What?" Miriam's eyes flew open; she gripped the edge of the table.

"Mrs. Wallace has volunteered to testify in court that your character is not as unblemished as it seems. In particu-lar, she's prepared to relate the details of the conversation I mentioned. It will become public knowledge that you feared you were with child out of wedlock at the age of six-teen."

Miriam's lips were pale, her face drawn. "This is a night-mare. Dr. Tanner assumes I'm . . . he assumes I've never had a beau, not a serious one. And a minister's wife must be above reproach, everyone knows that. If he finds out that I was . . . that Chet and I . . ."

"Is it true?" Nell asked. "Did you have Chet Langdon's baby?"

She hesitated a moment before looking away and say-ing, "No. No, I did not."

Will looked inquiringly toward Nell, as if wondering whether she believed the denial. Nell shrugged, not know-ing what to think. Call it what you will, circumspection or secretiveness, Miriam Bassett didn't tend to part easily with the truth.

"I was such an idiot," Miriam said. "Such a naïve little idiot. What must I have been thinking, to trust someone like Sophie?"

"After you confided in her," Will said, "she went to Munro and told him you were expecting."

"I knew it. I *knew* she must have said something to him. Why else would he have . . ." Groaning, Miriam propped her elbows on the table and cradled her head in her hands.

"She wanted him to think you were unworthy of marriage," Nell said. "That was why he stopped trying to court you."

"Yes, but you can't have been too displeased about that," Will said. "You said yourself, you had no interest in him—at the time."

Miriam raised her head from her hands. "At the time?"

"We know you've been calling on him at night over the summer," Nell said, "sneaking in through his back door and taking the service stairs up to his—"

"Those visits were entirely innocent," she said heatedly. "I . . . I was trying to talk him out of marrying Becky."

"Why?" Nell asked.

"*Why?* I . . . I've already told you why. It wasn't a betrothal, it was a . . . business transaction. Becky deserved better. She deserved a love match, not some cold-blooded union with someone she didn't even like."

"That was your father's reason for opposing the marriage," Will said. "What was yours?"

"I'm sure I've no idea what you mean."

"Were you jealous?" Nell asked.

"*Jealous?*" With a dubious little gust of laughter, she said, "You're daft—both of you."

"It must have made you more than a little angry as well," Nell said, "that Munro was toying with you while campaigning so zealously for your sister's hand in marriage. It must have stung, knowing he held you in such low regard, when he'd once tried so hard to make you his—"

"Get out." Miriam stood, knocking over her chair. "I've heard enough of this. Get out of my house." She marched to the door and pointed a quivering finger at it. "Get out right now."

"Miss Bassett," Nell began.

"Get out!" She slammed a fist against the wall for emphasis. "Get out, both of you! Who do you think you are, coming into my home and, and accusing me of—"

Rising, Will said, "My apologies if we—"

"I detest you, both of you!" she screamed, hot color scalding her face. "You're despicable! *Get out! Get out, damn you! Just get out!*"

Chapter 11

"I can't tell you how pleased I am that you're willing to have the surgery," Will told Eileen the next morning as he slid the crude but ingenious boot back onto her right leg. He had given her malformed foot a thorough examination, during which he'd asked Nell to make detailed pencil drawings of it from several angles, to be sent along with his letter to Dr. Sayre in New York.

"Here, let me," Eileen said as she leaned forward in Will's big leather desk chair to refasten the boot. "I made this thing, and can't nobody but me ever figger it out."

Will's office at the medical school, across from Massachusetts General Hospital, was rather small, but with two windows to let in the sun—not that there was much to let in this morning, with the sky heavily overcast. The floor-to-ceiling shelves lining the walls were crammed not just with books, but with jars housing an assortment of diseased body parts, worms, and the larval stages of various flies and beetles. Glass-fronted display cases, such as one might use for butterflies, held rows of carefully labeled bullets, both fresh and spent, alongside pinned-up sketches illustrating grisly wounds and dissected corpses. A reconstructed human skeleton wearing a top hat stood to one side of the big, cluttered desk. Eileen had found it all quite sickening, Nell fascinating.

It was strange, being here in Will's workplace, seeing this side of him—the forensic scientist, the teacher and researcher. She'd found herself marveling at how different he appeared here, in this enclave of medical academia, how changed from his former self, before remembering that this was exactly who William Hewitt had been before the war—a surgeon with a special interest in medical jurisprudence. He seemed completely at home here, in his masculine little office surrounded by his specimens and books; he seemed happy.

And yet, at the end of this term, he would be taking a train to San Francisco, and from there, a steamer to China.

Will had betrayed no hint since Sunday of any lingering disquiet from their conversation in his mother's garden, and neither of them had spoken of it. He'd asked her to forget about it, and Nell was trying to, or at least pretending to. It helped that she'd been occupied all day, with little time to ruminate on anything other than their inquiries into Philip Munro's death. Not so last night, when she'd lain awake in the dark, replaying his softspoken, heartstopping request for a kiss.

It was the first time in the year and a half of their

acquaintance that either of them had given voice to that which went unspoken between them. Part of Nell—the prudent, rational part, the part she showed the world—wished Will had never asked for that kiss. The other part—the young woman curled up in her too-big bed, waiting for the sheets to warm—ached to give him what he'd asked for, and more.

"Ye sure it won't cost me nothin'?" Eileen asked as she laced up the boot. "I haven't a copper penny to me name, 'cept what ya gave me th' other day."

Propping a hip on the edge of his desk, Will said, "Dr. Sayre's expenses and anything else not covered by the medical school will be borne by me. All you'll have to worry about is recuperating, and I'll make sure you've got plenty of help with that." Will's plan was to invite the renowned bone surgeon to Boston to demonstrate his technique for repairing clubfeet to the students and faculty of Harvard Medical School, the operation to be performed on Eileen.

"I know you're probably worried about losing your job because you won't be able to work for a while," said Nell as she deepened the shading on the front-view drawing. "Perhaps if Mrs. Hewitt speaks to Miss Bassett on your behalf, she'll consider—"

"Och, it don't matter no more," Eileen said. "I'm done with the Bassetts, and good riddance."

"You quit your job?" Nell asked.

"I'm fixin' to."

"But I thought you said they were the only people who would employ you."

"On account of me leg." Having secured the boot,

Eileen gave her foot a good stomp on the carpeted floor. "But if I ain't gonna be a cripple no more, or not so bad of one, maybe I can get me a better job, a payin' one. Father Gannon, he wants me out of there. He don't like . . . some of what I told him in confession."

Will gave Nell an interrogatory little glance, as if unsure whether it would do to question Eileen about something as delicate as her private communications with her priest. Reasoning that the girl wouldn't have brought it up if she hadn't wanted, on some level, to talk about it, Nell asked, "Do you mean your confession this past Sunday?"

Eileen nodded as she smoothed her skirts down, taking her time about it so as not to meet their gazes. "Not the bit about the surgery. Father was all for that. But I told him other things, things that happened Friday, and he said I'd been blackmailed into sinning, on account of lyin' is a sin—not just outright gum, but . . . th' other kind, where you know a thing but keep it to yerself."

"Gum?" Will asked.

"Lies," Nell said. "He's right," she told Eileen. "That kind of lie is a sin, too." Never mind that Nell's own lies of omission about her checkered past should guarantee her eons in Purgatory, if not worse.

"I did both kinds," Eileen said without looking up. "The regular kind and the keepin' it to yourself kind. I did me penance, but my soul still don't feel altogether clean, like it oughta. I think it's 'cause . . ." She glanced up at them, then down again. "It was yerselves I lied to, and now, with the two of ya bein' so kind and all, I feel like the Holy Father wants more from me than just a string of Hail Marys. I think He wants me to undo my sin."

"By telling us the truth?" Nell asked.

Looking up cautiously, Eileen nodded again.

Will said, "What you told us the other day, about Miss Bassett sending you for the key to her father's bedroom, and being with her when she discovered her father's body, was that . . ."

"That happened," Eileen said. "What I . . . left out was what happened before that."

"When Miss Bassett first came home from her errands?"

"No, before she left—only I ain't so sure it was errands she went out to do, exactly."

Not wanting anything omitted from Eileen's account this time, Nell said, "Why don't you start at the beginning? Presumably Friday started out like any other day. When did things start changing?"

"When Miss Bassett heard the newsboy yellin' 'Extra,' and sent me out to buy a copy."

"In the early afternoon, then," Will said.

"Aye, it was just as I'd finished cleanin' up from lunch. She had me bring the paper up to her da, and then I was holed up in the kitchen fer a spell, ironing the wash. I heard footsteps comin' down the stairs, real slow and heavy, so I knew it was himself, and not one of the sisters. I looked down the hall and saw him headin' out the front door in a good suit of clothes. Wasn't often I saw him that way, turned out all proper. Most days he just kept to his room in his shirtsleeves—sometimes just his nightshirt all day."

"Was he gone long?" Will asked.

Eileen frowned as she thought about it. "An hour? Maybe a little less. I was makin' me way up the service stairs with a stack of pressed linens, and I heard him on the landing of the main stairs—that landing with the big tall window that has them cracks in it."

"The one you can see from the front hall?" Nell asked.

"That's right. There's a door on that landing that opens onto the service stairs, and it ain't very thick. It's painted to look like mahogany, but it ain't, and ya can hear right through it when's somebody's talkin' loud on th' other side. Mr. Bassett, he had that big, deep voice, don't you know, and was goin' on about how he'd been ruined. Miss Bassett was there, too, and she was tryin' to shush him."

"The elder Miss Bassett?" Nell asked, just to make sure.

"That's right. She sounds a lot different than Miss Becky, so I knew it was her. Mr. Bassett's voice was shakin' so hard, it almost didn't sound like him. I knew it was wrong to stand there and listen, but if you'd heard him . . ." Eileen shook her head. "I liked him. Low-spirited as he was, he was always kind to me, never troubled me for much. He'd ask me how I was gittin' along, and were his daughters workin' me too hard. And here he was, carryin' on like that. I tell you, my heart bled for him."

"What did he say?" Will asked.

"He'd been to see some fella, and he was mad about somethin' the fella had done. He said, 'He did it on purpose—on *purpose*.' He kept repeating that bit—'on purpose.' He called the fella some names I don't want to say, which struck me odd, 'cause he wasn't the type to swear, 'specially in front of his girls. Miss Bassett, she was askin' him to get hold of himself, but he was only gittin' more worked up. The worst of it was when he started cryin'."

"Crying?" Nell asked.

"His voice had that wet, sobby kind of sound. I heard him say, 'He admitted it. He laughed about it.' Then he started in about somethin' else this fella had said. I couldn't make it out too good, on account of the cryin', but it had to do with Miss Bassett comin' to see him, and things she said to him."

"Said to Mr. Mun—the other fellow?" Nell asked.

"I think so. It was kind of hard to follow, 'cause of all the cryin'. Mr. Bassett says, 'I told him it's a foul lie, that you never would of said such a thing. Tell me he's just makin' it up.' Well, then *she* starts cryin', and she says it's the truth. And Mr. Bassett, he starts bellowin' somethin' fierce. Took the Lord's name in vain, and I never thought I'd see the day he done that. He asked her did anybody else know, and she said . . . I think it was Kathleen."

"Catherine?" Will asked.

"Catherine," Eileen said with a nod. "Miss Bassett, she says, 'Me and her talked about it Wednesday night, but she won't tell, 'cause she don't want nobody to know.' Then Mr. Bassett starts in about how this fella didn't just ruin *him,* he ruined his whole family. He says the fella ruined him just to prove he could, and that he'd . . . I think he said he'd 'give the fifty thousand back' if Mr. Bassett . . . it sounded like 'if I were to give my blessing.' "

"It means allowing Becky to marry," Nell said.

"Miss Becky's gettin' hitched?"

"Not anymore. What happened then?"

"There was more cryin' and talkin', and then Miss Bassett says, 'Don't worry, Papa. I'll take care of it. Everything will be all right.' "

"Take care of what?" Will asked.

Eileen shook her head. "I'm tellin' you what I could make out. She told him he should go lie down in his room, and that she'd fetch me and have me bring him a brandy. Sometimes, when she's lookin' fer me, she takes the service stairs, and sure enough the door flies open, and I'm face to face with her. Mr. Bassett was shufflin' away, he didn't notice, but Miss Bassett knew right off I'd been earwigging. She asked me what I heard, and I said not much, but she didn't believe me. She told me if I ever repeated any of it, she'd sack me with no references, and no one else would want me, on account of me leg."

Nell said, "I can't imagine Miriam Bassett making a threat like that. She's . . . I suppose you'd say self-contained, but she's never struck me as cruel. Not that I don't believe you, but . . ."

"She wasn't herself," Eileen said. "She was scared. I could tell. I told her I wouldn't say nothin' to no one, and then I brung Mr. Bassett his brandy. He was sittin' on the edge of his bed with his head hangin' down, all red-eyed. I asked him was anything wrong, but he didn't answer me." Sadly she added, "It was the last time I saw him alive."

"Where was Becky when all this was going on?" Nell asked.

"Out."

"Out where?"

Eileen shrugged. "She goes out visiting sometimes. There's a couple of young ladies in the neighborhood she's friendly with. Or sometimes she shops without buyin' nothin'. Miss Bassett went out after that, too. She had me to help her change her clothes. She'd been wearing that drab old frock she does chores in, and she needed me to lace her up tighter and button her into her striped walking dress."

"Yellow and pink stripes?" Nell asked. "With a ruffled skirt?"

"That's right. She put her bonnet and gloves on, too, so I knew she was goin' out."

"Did she say where she was going?" Will asked.

"Nah."

"Did you notice when she returned?"

"Yeah, I was scrubbin' the floor in the front hall when she come in. She never even looked at me, just raced up them stairs, white as a sheet. A minute later she calls down to me to fetch the key to her da's room from the butler's pantry, so I did."

"And the rest is as you told us the other day?" Nell asked. "Unlocking the room and finding Mr. Bassett with his wrists cut?"

"Aye . . ." she said hesitantly. " 'Cept for one more thing I kinda . . . didn't mention, and one . . . well, one real lie, the outright kind."

"Let's hear the outright one first," Will said.

Eileen literally covered her face in shame. "You remember when you asked me if I'd found a note and I said no?"

"You did find one?" Nell asked.

The girl lowered her hands enough to meet Nell's eyes, and nodded. "Miss Bassett asked me to look for one. I found it on his pillow and gave it to her."

"Did she give you any indication of what it said?" Nell

asked, knowing what the answer would be, but not wanting to assume.

Eileen shook her head. "Sorry. She started tearin' up when she read it, but she didn't say what was in it. She told me I must keep it their secret, about there bein' a note, otherwise I'd get the sack and all that, and then she went to her room. I heard her sobbing past candle lighting."

"And you never saw the note again?" Will asked. "When you cleaned her room, perhaps?"

"Sorry, no.

"What was the lie of omission?" Nell asked.

"The keepin' it to yerself kind? It was about Miss Bassett's dress, the one she changed into to go out. After she come back and had me fetch the key, I noticed . . ." Eileen glanced at Nell and Will, then lowered her voice along with her gaze. "I was standin' behind her when she unlocked the door, and . . . it was buttoned wrong."

"Her dress?" Nell asked.

Eileen nodded. "It buttons down the back, and there was a button that got skipped—you know, so there's a little gap, and then the rest of the buttons are one buttonhole off? The thing of it is, she was buttoned up perfect when she left the house. I should know. I did it meself."

"Which would suggest," Nell said, "that, between leaving the house and coming home, she removed her dress and put it back on."

"Which, in turn," Will said, "would suggest how Miss Bassett meant to 'take care of' the problem of her family's impoverishment without condemning her sister to a loveless marriage—a marriage to the man with whom she may, in fact, have been smitten herself."

"She offered herself in Becky's stead?" Nell asked.

"He'd apparently been trying to seduce her all summer. According to Harry, he'd become obsessed with having her . . . on his own terms."

"But would he have accepted a Bassett mistress in lieu of a Bassett bride?" Nell asked. "Would Miriam have been worth fifty grand to him?"

"From what we know of the man," Will said, "I wouldn't put it past him to let Miriam follow through with her end of the deal, then renege on his."

"I . . . I don't think so," Eileen said.

Nell and Will turned to look at the pink-faced girl, whose blush deepened as she said, "I mean I don't think Miss Bassett . . . did what you think she did with that fella. I don't think that's why her dress was buttoned wrong."

"Why *do* you think it was buttoned wrong, then?" Nell asked.

"I dunno, but I don't think it was that."

"Why not?" Will asked.

Eileen ducked her head and shrugged.

Will said, "If you're holding something back—"

"It's just . . ." She glanced at him, then quickly away. "Fergit it. I'm just blatherin'. I don't know nothin'."

"Is it that you don't think wellborn, churchgoing ladies do that sort of thing?" Nell asked. "Or is it because she's engaged to Dr. Tanner?"

"I . . . I reckon I don't know. Like I said, I'm blatherin'."

"Miriam Bassett is a person who does what needs to be done," Nell said. "Or what she thinks needs to be done. If she felt there was no alternative, I think she might have committed a sin for the sake of her family."

"I s'pose so," Eileen said, but she didn't sound convinced.

"MISS Munro is not at home," declared the sour-faced butler with the black armband who opened the door to Nell and Will later that morning.

Nell considered and rejected the notion of saying, *We know she's at home, you self-important little toad. We saw her in the front window of her brother's office as we were walking up to the house.* Catherine Munro had looked like a black-clad wraith, staring out through the swath of crepe with her white face and her sad eyebrows and her vague, dreamy gaze. A skyful of clouds, dark as smoke, cast an appropriately murky pall over the scene.

"Not at home" usually meant "not at home for callers" or "not at home for particular callers." After their last visit, which had left the late Mr. Munro's fourth-floor office in shambles, Nell suspected his sister had issued orders that they never again be allowed into her home.

"Would you ask Miss Munro if she would be so kind as to make an exception and see us?" Will asked. "It's a matter of some importance."

"I'm afraid that's out of the question, sir. Mr. Munro's funeral is to take place this afternoon, and Miss Munro prefers to be undisturbed until then."

Having been thus dismissed, Nell and Will walked a few doors down to an alley between two blocks of attached townhouses, wove their way to the kitchen yard of the Munro house, and opened the back door after a perfunctory knock. Doffing his hat, Will said good morning to Mrs. Gell and her slow-witted assistant, and escorted Nell up the skylit service stairs.

They entered Philip Munro's office to find Catherine still standing with her back to them at the middle bay window. The room was unlit but for a meager haze of sunlight through the filmy crepe. If Nell hadn't known that the shadowy form by the window was Catherine, she might have thought no one was there.

"I'm not at home," Catherine said without turning around. Her voice, naturally soft, had an especially blurry quality this morning.

Will said, "We realize that, Miss Munro, and I apologize for the imposition, but we have something important to ask you that may help to unravel the truth about how your brother died. You'll be burying him this afternoon. Perhaps, by then, we'll have disproved the notion that he died by his own hand, which will perhaps provide you some comfort as you lay him to rest. I promise we won't take up any more of your time than absolutely necessary."

Catherine remained entirely motionless for so long that Nell had decided she was unmoved by Will's handsome speech . . . until she slowly turned toward them. As she did so, her gaze fell on a small druggist's vial on the window ledge, before Catherine scooped it into a hidden pocket in her dress. It was another elegantly unfussy crepe gown, this one sans weeping cuffs and with a very high neck that framed her chin in tiny black pleats. There were no buttons or adornments of any kind, no belt buckle, no key ring, no watch—just a wasp-waisted silhouette of matte black punctuated by the glittery little locket housing Philip Munro's portrait.

Catherine's face and hands looked unnaturally pale against the darkness of her hair and dress and the surrounding room. Nell took a mental photograph so that she could capture the image later in India ink brushed onto good, heavy watercolor paper with just a hint of a tooth.

"What is your question?" Catherine asked, her hands clasped at her waist, her eyes oddly heavy-lidded.

Moving farther into the room, Nell saw that some of the damage Harry had wreaked with that cricket bat had been repaired. There were new sheets of glass over the pictures on the wall, and new shelves on the étagère. The silk wallpaper, however, bore an unsightly grayish abrasion where someone had tried to scrub away the ink stain; it would need to be replaced.

"What we'd like to know," Nell told her, "is what Miriam Bassett talked to you about Wednesday night."

Catherine frowned blearily. "Wednesday night?"

"She spoke to you about something," Will said. "It was something she'd told your brother, something of a confidential nature. Friday afternoon, your brother shared it with Mr. Bassett, who didn't believe it at first. When he found out it was true, he became very distraught. It would go far toward helping us piece together what happened that day if we knew what it was Miss Bassett spoke to you about."

"Have you asked *her*?"

"We thought you might be more forthcoming," Nell said.

"You thought wrong," Catherine said. "Philip's posthumous reputation is all he has left. It is my intent to promote that reputation through philanthropic works in his name, not sully it."

"So it's something that reflects poorly upon your brother," Nell said. "Then I can certainly understand why you might want to keep such information to yourself, but you should know what the repercussions will be, should you take that tack. Dr. Hewitt and I will have to expand our investigation, question many more people. If we do that, certain other information is bound to get around, information that, if I were you, I might want to keep under wraps."

"Such as?"

"Such as the fact that Philip Munro took advantage of his power of attorney on behalf of Noah Bassett to destroy Mr. Bassett financially."

Catherine said, "If Mr. Bassett suffered setbacks Friday, that is most regretful, I'm sure, but it is hardly my brother's fault. Countless investors were ruined Friday."

"How many were ruined," Will asked, "as a result of the deliberate connivance of their advisors?"

"That's absurd," Catherine said.

"It's the truth," Nell said, "Your brother talked Mr. Bassett into buying gold with borrowed money, and left him holding it Friday when he knew the market was about to collapse. His purpose was to force Mr. Bassett to allow his marriage to Becky. If he allowed it, your brother would dig him out of the hole he'd dropped him in. If not . . ." She lifted her shoulders. "I suppose Noah Bassett would have ended his days in the poor house."

Catherine said, "You can't prove any of this."

"We have telegrams taken from your brother's safe that will prove it quite effectively."

Catherine's eyes glowed as if they were lit from within. "You took things belonging to my brother?"

"You can have them back when the district attorney is through with them," Nell said. "You do realize it's not just unethical, but an actual criminal act to abuse a power of attorney that way. Noah Bassett was a beloved figure in this city. When it becomes known what was done to him, your brother will be forever remembered as a duplicitous, double-crossing schemer."

"You might consider naming the Philip James Munro Foundation after someone else," Will said dryly.

Catherine stood with her eyes closed for a moment, then walked to the chaise lounge, her layers of black crepe whispering *shush, shush, shush* in the dusky room. She sat and folded her hands in her lap, staring at nothing. "If I tell you about . . . Wednesday night," she said in a voice almost devoid of inflection, "who will find out?"

Will said, "That would depend, I suppose, on what you tell us, and how helpful it is in explaining your brother's murder. All I can promise, but it is a sincere gentleman's promise, is that I'll be as vigilant as possible in keeping certain information, such as your brother's dealings with Mr. Bassett, out of the Boston gossip mill."

Catherine's chest rose and fell slowly. In a somnolent monotone, she said, "Miriam came to see him Wednesday night. I knew she was up here. I heard raised voices, but I ignored them. Philip needs his—*needed* his privacy. I tended to turn a deaf ear to what went on up here."

Will exchanged a grim look with Nell. No doubt he, too, was recalling what his brother had said about Munro's ravishment of Sophie. *I was sure someone would come upstairs to see what the ruckus was, but nobody did.*

"Finally," Catherine said, "I heard Miriam's feet on the stairs, but instead of going out the back door, she came and found me in my sewing room. She said she knew I didn't like her, and that she didn't much care for me, either, but that I'd want to hear what she had to say. She said she was giving up on trying to get through to Philip. She'd been trying all summer, but he was being thick, and even though she'd promised herself long ago that she'd never tell anyone, she'd finally broken down and told Philip, and now she had to tell me, because Philip didn't believe her, and if anyone could convince him, it would be I."

Catherine shut her eyes and rubbed her temples with tremulous fingers.

Will rolled Munro's leather chair from behind the desk and offered it to Nell, who sat. Leaning back against the big desk, arms crossed, he said, "Was this the first time you realized Miss Bassett's visits to your brother were platonic in nature? That she was merely trying to . . . 'get through to him'?"

Catherine nodded with her eyes still closed, fingertips kneading her temples. "Philip never discussed his women with me. He had too much . . ." She sighed. *He had too much respect for me.* That was what she'd told them the other day. Nell wondered if she still believed it.

"What did Miriam tell you?" Nell asked.

"She said she needed my help in keeping Philip from marrying Rebecca. I assumed she was opposed to the marriage on the basis of Philip's low birth, so I lied and told her I didn't care if they got married, in fact I was all in favor of it. She asked me . . . she asked me if I would still feel that way if I knew that Rebecca wasn't really Noah Bassett's child, that she'd been fathered by someone else. I told her it wouldn't make any difference to me, but that it was a vile affront to her mother to say such a thing, true or not. So she said . . ."

Catherine wrapped a hand around the locket. "She said that Rebecca wasn't really her mother's child, either, that her mother hadn't given birth to her—that she, Miriam, had, when she was sixteen. And she said that the reason we must do everything possible to prevent the marriage was because . . ." Catherine looked up wanly, her gaze lighting on Will, then Nell. "Because Philip was Rebecca's father."

Chapter 12

WILL crossed to the cocktail cabinet and poured three stiff brandies. Catherine drank half of hers fairly quickly, then lay back on the chaise, looking exhausted. "Do you want to hear the whole—"

"Yes," Nell and Will said in unison.

"This all happened some twenty years ago, and I didn't follow Philip to Boston till 'fifty-seven, so all I know is what Miriam told me Wednesday night. She said she'd had a beau when she was young who went to Europe, Chet something."

"Langdon, I think it was," Nell said.

"Philip had been trying to court her, too, around the same time, but she'd been discouraging him, undoubtedly because of his lack of lineage. Anyway, Miriam had allowed Chet to compromise her before he took ship, and

Philip found out about it. Of course, now that he knew what kind of female Miriam was, he abandoned the notion of marrying her, but he was still, well, a man. He had Sophie. She was his mistress. But he also had a masculine drive to pursue and conquer, so . . ."

It was an indication of Catherine's obsession with her late brother, Nell thought, that her recounting of these events should be from his perspective rather than that of the person who'd related them to her.

Catherine drank some more brandy, looking preoccupied. "The gist of it is that Philip pursued and conquered Miriam Bassett. Sometime afterward, Miriam realized she was in a delicate condition—by Philip, not Chet. Of course, she never thought to give Philip the chance to do the right thing and marry her. She never even told him she was with child, that's how contemptuous she was of his social standing. Instead, she went to spend her confinement with relatives in New York under the guise of taking the yearlong finishing course at Miss Finch's. Meanwhile, her mother feigned a pregnancy by padding her dresses, and when Miriam returned with baby Rebecca, Mrs. Bassett reared her as her own."

Catherine had known all this the last time they spoke, Nell realized, but all she'd told them was that Miriam was virulently opposed to the marriage, not why. She'd wanted them to suspect that Miriam might have had something to do with her brother's death, while concealing the fact that he'd come perilously close to marrying his own daughter.

"Her father knew the truth, didn't he?" Nell asked.

"He knew that Rebecca was Miriam's daughter, but not

that she'd been fathered by Philip. His wife had made Miriam promise never to tell him, for fear that he might come to blows with Philip. I don't have to tell you who would have prevailed in such an encounter. Philip was a strapping man, well-versed in fisticuffs from Harvard, and quite a bit younger than Mr. Bassett."

"Does Becky know?" Will asked.

"Oh, good heavens, no. Say what you will about Miriam Bassett, but she's no fool. She knew that if she ever told that yammering little bag of wind the truth, it would be all over Boston in the blink of an eye, and their reputations would be in tatters. No, as far as Becky knows, she's the legitimate daughter of Noah and Lucy Bassett. Miriam didn't even dare tell her after Philip started courting her, because she knew Rebecca would blurt it out to the wrong person sooner or later. Miriam seemed particularly concerned that her fiancé not find out about all this. He's a clergyman, I take it. No idea what kind of woman he's really marrying, poor man."

"I take it you tried to talk your brother out of marrying Becky after that," Nell said. *She was fit to be tied,* Harry had said. *Crying, wailing . . . "You can't do this! It's unspeakable!"*

"Philip wouldn't accept that he was Rebecca's father. He insisted Miriam was already expecting when he and she . . ." Catherine waved a desultory hand. "I wasn't so sure. You see, it was Sophie who'd told him about Miriam being with child. She's never been what you'd call the trustworthy type, not to mention her unwholesome attachment to my brother."

If ever a pot had called a kettle black, Nell thought.

* * *

"EILEEN! The door!"

Nell, standing next to Will on the Bassetts' front stoop later that morning, could not have been more surprised when the door was opened by Eileen herself.

"Och, Miss Sweeney. Dr. Hewitt. Come in, come in."

"Have you given your notice yet?" asked Will, sotto voce, as they stepped into the front hall.

"I'll be doin' that right before the surgery. You're here to see Miss Bassett and Miss Becky, I suspect."

"Just Miss Bassett this time," Will said.

"She and Dr. Tanner went over to that church on Newbury to see the pastor that's gonna do the funeral this afternoon, but they should be back presently. Miss Becky, she's up in her room readin' one of them dime novels. Ye can wait in the parlor if you want. Mr. Bassett ain't laid out in there no more. They went and took him over to the church already."

Nell said, "There's actually something I'd like to ask you first, if we can speak privately." To Will she said, "I'll join you in a minute."

"Of course," replied Will, whom Nell had told to expect this.

He retreated to the parlor, Nell and Eileen to the dining room. Closing the door behind them, Nell said, "Yesterday morning, when we were talking about Miss Bassett's dress being buttoned wrong, you were adamant that she and the gentleman she'd been visiting hadn't been intimate, but you couldn't tell me why you felt that way. I've been thinking about it, and it strikes me that you might feel more comfortable discussing this without Dr. Hewitt present."

Eileen, her face blooming with color, mumbled, "I . . . reckon so."

"You can be candid with me," Nell assured her. "There's nothing you can say that would shock me. Why is it that you think Miss Bassett hadn't been with him that way?"

Her head down, apron twisted in her hands, Eileen said, "Not that I'd know fer sure, but from what I've heard, you know, from them that have husbands . . . I might be wrong, but, well, ya don't really want to be . . . doin' that sort of thing when you're . . . you know . . . unwell. Do ya?"

"Ah. Well, one can, but many ladies prefer not to. Do you have some reason to think Miss Bassett was having her monthlies?"

Reddening even more, Eileen said, "I went up to lay out her bedclothes Friday night, not thinkin' she was in her room, 'cause she likes to read in the parlor before she turns in. 'Course, Friday wasn't like other days, but I had so much on me mind after all that'd happened, and . . . well, I just barged into her room without even knockin'. She'd already changed fer bed, and she was gatherin' up the clothes she'd worn that day . . ."

"The yellow and pink striped walking dress?" Nell asked.

"Aye, and her . . . unmentionables. She jumped when she saw me, and she turned 'round real quick, but I seen what she was holdin'—just for a second, but I seen it well enough to know it was her time of the month."

"You saw blood?" Nell asked.

Eileen nodded.

"On her underthings?"

"On them and on the dress, too. She'd turned it inside out, and I seen there was a little on the inside of the skirt. A terrible lot on her petticoat, though."

"Did she give you those things to wash?" Nell asked.

"Nah, she dumped it all in the dye pot the next morning. Well, not the crinoline. I think she musta managed to get the blood outa that, 'cause she's been wearin' it since then, and it looks fine to me. And the dress didn't take the dye too good, so she gave that to the rag picker. But I know she dyed some of them underthings—I reckon on account of the bloodstains."

"I reckon so," Nell said.

" So that was why she wouldn't discuss it in front of me," Will said with an amused little shake of the head after Nell had joined him in the parlor and. "Too embarrassed to mention the female cycle in the presence of a physician, eh?"

Easy for Will to scoff. Nell, her pragmatic nature and nursing experience notwithstanding, had had to steel herself to relate Eileen's observations to Will. It just wasn't a subject for a gentleman's ears, doctor or no.

"The thing of it is," Nell said, hoping he didn't notice the heat rising in her cheeks, "I'm not altogether sure that the blood Eileen saw had anything to do with . . . female matters."

"Indeed."

"Eileen said there was quite a bit of it on Miriam's petticoat. In order get there, it would have had to, well, soak through her drawers and crinoline first—assuming it really was . . . that kind of blood. It probably would have also stained the bottom part of her shimmy. But oddly enough, none of those things made it into the dye pot."

"She did, however, dye her corset and corset cover."

"Curious," Nell murmured.

"Yes, quite."

MIRIAM, who returned home about twenty minutes later, accompanied by Dr. Tanner, was understandably irate upon finding Nell and Will sitting in her front parlor, given her furious ousting of them the day before. She adamantly refused to speak to them privately.

"I have nothing to say to you," she told them. "Please leave now, or I shall be forced to summon a constable."

"If you won't speak to us," Nell said, "we'll go from here directly to the Detectives' Bureau at City Hall and tell them some things I feel quite certain you would rather we didn't."

Miriam sent her fiancé from the room and closed the door. "I know you think you have it all sorted out," she said as she turned to face them. "You think I was smitten with Philip Munro, and that was why I wanted to keep him away from Becky. You think I was so maddened by jealousy that I murdered him rather than let him marry my sister, but believe me, nothing could be further from the truth."

"We know that now," Nell said. "We also know it wasn't Chet Langdon's baby you had when you were sixteen—it was Mr. Munro's."

"And you opposed the marriage not out of jealousy,"

Will added, "but because you couldn't permit your daughter to marry her own father."

The color leached from Miriam's face; she put a hand to her stomach, swaying slightly. Will crossed to her in two long strides and lowered her gently into a threadbare armchair. Nell poured her a glass of red wine from a carafe in a cupboard.

Miriam's color returned as she drank the wine, almost as if it were going directly to her cheeks.

Will said, "It's true, I take it. Philip Munro fathered Becky."

"How did you find out? From Catherine Munro?" Miriam looked thoughtful as she set the half-empty wineglass on a little marble-topped table. "It must have been Catherine. No one else knows. With Mamá gone, it's just been me keeping the secret, so I never fretted about it. But now . . ." Leaning her elbows on her knees, she buried her face in her hands. "What else do you know?"

Will said, "We know that your father came home Friday afternoon with the news that Munro had ruined him in order to force his approval of the marriage. If he blessed it, he'd get the fifty thousand back. If he didn't, he'd remain an impoverished debtor. You had an excruciating choice to make. You couldn't allow the marriage, but you also couldn't allow your father to end up in the poor house."

"As usual," Nell said, "it was all up to you. For months, Philip Munro, apparently eager to rekindle your affair of twenty years ago, had been trying to seduce you. So you went to him and offered yourself in return for his breaking it off with Becky and giving the fifty thousand back to your father. He let you fulfill your end of the bargain, but afterward, in true Philip Munro style, he told you nothing had changed. Either he'd end up married to Becky, or your father would end up ruined. You were seething. You'd debased yourself for nothing. In a blind rage, you smashed him over the head with one of his own cricket bats, then heaved him out the window to make it look like suicide."

"You assumed the gold crash would provide a motive for his having taken his life," Will added, "little knowing he'd sailed through it unscathed."

"Unfortunately, when you got home," Nell said, "you found your father dead by his own hand, and a note from him explaining that he had nothing left but his life insurance—his parting gift to his daughters."

Miriam, still hunched over with her head in her hands, was shaking uncontrollably.

"Miss Bassett?" Nell said.

She looked up, her arms banded around herself, face wet. "I hadn't known about the insurance," she said in a voice rusty with tears. "Neither had Becky. Not until the note."

"What happened to the note?" Will handed her a handkerchief, but she just wadded it up in her hand.

"I b-burned it."

"Why?"

"It was the least I could do."

"I don't understand," Nell said. "Why was it the—"

"It should have been me. I wish it had been me. It was my doing. If I h-hadn't had Eileen bring him that extra, if I'd only been *thinking*, he never would have . . . he wouldn't have—" She broke off on a sob.

Nell looked toward Will, but he didn't seem to be on any firmer ground that she.

Miriam bolted out of the chair and flung the door open.

"Miss Bassett!" Dr. Tanner, standing on the other side of the door, caught her in his arms as she fled from the room. "What the . . ."

Miriam said something through her sobs as she strove to wrestle out of his grip, but it was unintelligible. "Easy . . ." Tanner soothed. Shifting his gaze to Nell and Will, he asked, "What the devil happened?"

Nell, at a loss, looked to Will. Seeming no more sure of himself than she, he said, "It would appear that Miss Bassett . . . We believe she was involved in the death of Phillip Munro."

"What?" It came out on an incredulous little flutter of laughter. "You can't be serious."

"She's not denying it," Will said.

"She's not capable of denying anything right now," Tanner said. "Look at her. She's beside herself." Leading her back into the parlor, he lowered her into the armchair she'd just leapt out of, took out his handkerchief, and gently blotted her face. "How reassuring to see you produce tears," Tanner told his fiancée with a mild smile. "Your self-composure has always been a bit unnerving."

This curious observation actually seemed to calm Miriam down a bit. She looked at Dr. Tanner as if she'd never seen him before in her life.

"I know you didn't kill Philip Munro," Tanner told her as he crouched down next to her. "You're incapable of taking a human life. Anything else you may have done, either recently or in the far past, is just part of who you are, part of the person I love and want to spend the rest of my life with. So, why won't you just tell us what happened Friday so that we can put all this nonsense behind us and move on?"

"It . . . it's because of Papa," Miriam said.

"Your father is gone," Tanner said. "Nothing you say can hurt him now."

"It can hurt his memory, and that's all that's left of him. How can I do that after everything he did for me?"

"I knew Noah Bassett fairly well," Tanner said, "and one thing I know for sure is that he would have been horrified to think of you suffering because of something he did. He always believed in taking responsibility for one's own actions. Let him do that now."

Miriam closed her eyes and gave a slight nod. A tear slid down her cheek. Tanner brushed it away, lightly caressing her face before withdrawing his hand.

"Early in the afternoon," Nell said, "you sent Eileen out to buy an extra about the gold crash from the newsboy, and you had her bring it up to your father."

"I never should have done that, given his state of mind," Miriam said. "I was busy. I wasn't thinking. It's my fault that he became so distraught."

"He got dressed and went to see Philip Munro then, yes?" Nell prompted.

Miriam said, "I didn't realize he was doing that, or I would have tried to stop him. I was upstairs when he came home, and I met him on the landing. He told me we were ruined, that we were going to lose the house. He said Philip had done it on purpose, and that he'd only fix it if Papa blessed his marriage to Becky. Papa refused. Some very hot words were exchanged. Munro asked him whom he thought he'd been dealing with. He told Papa he'd send him to the poor house, then set Becky up as his mistress, and when he was done with her, he'd sell her to some Fort Hill brothel. He said . . ." Miriam looked at Tanner, then at the floor. "He said some things about me, too, things Papa hadn't known before. Papa . . . he said it was as if were watching himself from above. He grabbed a cricket bat off the rack, and . . ."

She was trembling. Tanner, kneeling beside her, chafed her hands.

"Papa said he couldn't believe it when he realized what he'd done. He said it felt unreal, as if another man had done it. He came straight home. He wanted to turn himself in to the police, but I begged him not to. I asked him if anyone had seen him enter Philip's house or leave it, and he said no, just that kitchen girl who never seems to notice anything. He was in tears, he was so upset. I'd never seen him like that. I told him I'd take care of it, and I sent Eileen to his room to bring him a brandy. I changed and went to Marlborough Street and slipped up the service stairs. Philip was slumped over his desk with his head all . . ." She shivered. "It was . . . it was . . ."

"It's all right, Miriam," murmured Dr. Tanner as he closed his hands around both of her. "I'm here." *Miriam.* It was the first time Nell had heard him call her by her Christian name.

"I didn't want to get blood all over my dress," Miriam said, "so I took it off before I started cleaning things up. I dragged Philip to the window and heaved him out, and then I got my dress back on as quickly as I could. I was wiping up the last few spots on the rug when I heard some-one outside, a man, say, 'Oh, my God.' "

"That would have been Freddie Wallace," Will said.

"There was a great deal of fuss out front then," Miriam said. "I had no trouble getting out the back door unseen. When I got home, I went straight upstairs to see Papa, but his bedroom door was locked. I knew right away some-thing was wrong. I had Eileen bring the key. It was the most awful thing I'd ever seen."

"What did he say in his note?" Nell asked.

"That he'd killed Philip Munro, on his own with no help from anyone else, and that he took full responsibility for it, both in this life and the next. He asked that the po-lice be informed of what he'd done so as to set the record straight."

"That sounds like Noah," Tanner said.

"He asked us to pray for both him and Philip," Miriam said. "And he said we—Becky and I—wouldn't have to worry about money from now on, because he had that life insurance."

"You dyed your bloodstained clothing," Nell said, "and burned the note. What happened to the cricket bat?"

"I smuggled it back home under my skirt and threw it in the kitchen fire before I went to check on Papa."

"Why were you so determined to erase all evidence of the connection between Philip Munro and your family?" Will asked.

"I thought if it came out that he'd helped Papa with his investments, eventually someone would discover that he'd ruined Papa."

"Thus giving your father a motive for killing him," Nell said.

"I just wanted to pretend he'd never existed."

"Yes, but if he hadn't," Tanner said quietly, "you never would have had Becky."

Miriam turned to stare at him. So did Nell and Will. When, Nell wondered, had Tanner come to realize that Becky was Munro's daughter.

"You opposed the marriage with such uncharacteristic virulence," Tanner told Miriam, "that I knew there must be more to the story than you were letting on. Then came the revelation that Munro had once wanted to marry you. And then this Sophie Wallace, née Cabot, who delights in spreading rumors about you that you would rather I didn't hear— which was why you sent me on that fool's errand to find Becky yesterday." The minister smiled at his fiancée. "My imagination can fill in a great deal, Miriam. I may be a man of the cloth, but I am vaguely acquainted, if only in an abstract sense, with the ways of the world."

That little speech actually drew a smile, albeit a small and rather wobbly one, from Miriam.

"Were you in love with Munro?" Tanner asked her.

"God, no. No! Never! He was never . . ." Miriam shook her head as if to settle her thoughts. "I had a beau, Chet Langdon. He was the one I . . . thought I loved. We were betrothed—secretly, because I was only sixteen, and Mamá would never have permitted it. I knew Philip wanted to take Chet's place—he'd made that abundantly clear—but I never gave him a second's encouragement. Chet and I . . . He was leaving for Europe the next day, and he was going to be gone a year, and he wanted . . . He, he said it was almost as if we were married already, and I, I already missed him so much . . ."

"Yes," Tanner said. "I understand."

"Afterward, I was worried about, well, getting in trouble. The only woman I knew who might know about these matters was Sophie Cabot. I had no idea she and Philip . . . If I did, I never would have confided in her. I wasn't pregnant, of course, just naïve and fretful. Sophie told Philip that I was carrying Chet's child, so of course he completely changed his mind about me. He came to think of me as a woman who gave herself cheaply, and when I resisted his advances, he . . . It was at the Children's Aid Ball. He put something in my champagne—I realized that later. Everything became . . . very strange. The room was whirling like a carousel, and I could barely stand. I remember being walked down a long hallway, being half-carried, really, and told I looked faint and needed to lie down, and then the next thing I remember is being on a couch in some little room, with my dress half undone, and him . . ." She shuddered.

Tanner swore under his breath and wrapped an arm around her.

"He knew I would never tell," Miriam said. "It would have destroyed my reputation. A few weeks later, my mother was having tea with Chet's mother, and she couldn't stop bragging about the young countess he was courting. By then, I knew I was pregnant by Philip Munro."

"I think I can guess what happened then," Tanner said. "Your mother sent you away under the pretext of finishing school and pretended she herself was with child. You returned to Boston after Becky was born, and no one was the wiser."

"That's right. I've never wanted to tell Becky, because she's such a chatterbox. I only told Philip because I had to prevent the wedding, no matter what it took, but he didn't believe me. He was convinced I'd already been with child by Chet when he . . . 'took his turn' with me. That was how he put it. I kept going back to see him, hoping I could talk sense to him—with my father's pistol in my pocket, just to feel safe. It was terribly frustrating trying to reason with him. All he seemed interested in was, well, having his way with me again. He was constantly making advances, switching tactics whenever it became clear that he wasn't getting anywhere. He assured me I didn't need the pistol, that he wouldn't do anything I didn't ask him to do, and that I *would* ask him sooner or later, that I'd end up begging him, in fact."

"*Begging* him?" Tanner said.

"His arrogance was almost laughable."

Having all too much insight into men like Philip Munro—there was a bit of him in Duncan—Nell said, "He was thinking that if the woman he'd once taken by force actually begged him for it, if she wanted it as much as he, it might mitigate what he'd done twenty years ago. A ravisher he may have been, but it would appear he didn't like to think of himself as such."

"I can't pretend I'm sorry that he's gone," Miriam said. "I *am* sorry that my father was the instrument of his death. Perhaps . . . perhaps I should do as he asked, and tell the police how Philip really died."

"If you do that," Nell said, "you will, of course, be implicating yourself. After all, you tampered with a murder scene for the purpose of misleading the authorities."

Will said, "Yes, but since she was merely trying to protect her father, I can't imagine her punishment, if there is any, will be very severe."

"It would be worth it," Miriam said, "just to have it all out in the open. I could be at peace with it, then." She looked at Dr. Tanner, took his hand. "I could start over."

NELL and Will were walking up the Bassetts' driveway toward his phaeton parked around back when she noticed a movement in the side parlor window: John Tanner clasping Miriam's arms, his head bent to hers as he spoke. Circling around to the passenger side of the black buggy, Nell stole a long look in their direction.

Miriam said something; Tanner nodded. He raised his hands to her face, framing it tenderly. She closed her eyes. He touched his mouth to her forehead, her eyelids, whispered earnestly in her ear . . .

Something brushed Nell's arm. She turned to find Will standing beside her, looking toward the window. He watched for a long moment, seeming deep in thought.

His gaze shifted to Nell. She had the impression he wanted to say something, but he didn't. He opened the carriage door and handed her up. They drove away in silence.

Four Months Later:
January 1870

❧

"ALL aboard for Providence and points west!" roared the railroad conductor through a speaking trumpet as he picked his way among the swarm of passengers, well-wishers, porters, and luggage carts jostling each other on the station platform. Steam from the waiting locomotive billowed into the frigid morning air.

Nell buttoned her coat with one gloved but numb hand and used the other to shield her eyes from the sun as she wove her way through the chaos, looking for Will. Her ears, only partially covered by her winter beret—aquamarine velvet, to match her coat collar—stung with the cold. Frozen slush crunched underfoot as she quickened her pace, searching, searching . . .

"With connections to the Union Pacific and the Central Pacific!"

She would never find him before he left on his self-imposed exile to the Orient. There were too many people; she'd come too late. It was bedlam.

"Chicago, Omaha, Cheyenne . . ."

She shouldn't have come. She'd promised herself she wouldn't, but then, at the last minute . . .

"Great Salt Lake City, Sacramento, Stockton, and *San . . . Fran . . . cisco!*"

As autumn surrendered to winter, Nell had entertained the hope that Will might change his mind about Shanghai. She'd avoided bringing it up, as if the idea might simply evaporate if only they didn't talk about it. For the most part, she was able to put it out of her mind altogether, occupied as she'd been these past months with caring for Gracie and helping Eileen Tierney through her surgery and recovery.

At Will's invitation, and funded by him, the renowned Dr. Lewis Albert Sayre had come to Boston to demonstrate his innovative new clubfoot operation in the surgical theater at Massachusetts General. Having left the Bassetts' employ, Eileen recuperated at the Hewitts' in a third-floor room near the nursery, so that Nell could look after her. She took so well to Gracie that Viola asked her to stay on as a sort of assistant to Nell—replacing the increasingly infirm Nurse Parrish—with the understanding that she would eventually serve as Gracie's lady's maid. Now entirely healed from the surgery, and with a lovely pair of custom-made boots Viola had ordered for her, Eileen's gait was so graceful that one would never suspect she'd been born with a deformity.

The reaction of upper-class Bostonians, when told the

circumstances of Philip Munro's murder, was nearly always the same. Poor Noah Bassett, it was felt, had been laboring under an aberration of mind when he took that cricket bat to Munro, who'd invited such a fate through his own rapaciousness. Around dinner tables at the Somerset Club and the Parker House, it was generally agreed that this sort of unseemly business was what came of elevating the lower classes. The district attorney, taking into account the extenuating circumstances and Miriam Bassett's standing in society—not to mention the support of the entire Brahmin community—declined to charge her as an accessory after the fact. She and John Tanner were married in October—in a small, quiet service, given that she was in mourning—and last week she'd confided to Nell that she was expecting.

"All aboard!"

She saw him.

Nell stopped walking and stared at him, her breath puff-puff-puffing. He was about twenty yards away, standing gravely still amid the roiling masses, his ubiquitous black top hat shadowing his eyes.

Will tugged off his gloves, stuffed them in a pocket of his great coat, and withdrew his tin of Bull Durhams. He studied it for a moment, flipped it open, tapped a cigarette, and lit it.

What was it he'd said, that he only lit up nowadays as a sort of nerve tonic? *Something to soothe me and keep me occupied when I can't quite abide the world and my role in it.*

Will held the smoke for a long moment, expelling it in a plume that hovered like a cloud in the blistering cold air.

Shoving one hand in a coat pocket, he looked around absently as he brought the cigarette to his mouth again.

He saw her and stilled.

He lowered the cigarette without drawing on it and strode toward her, black coat and gray silk scarf flapping behind him.

Nell shivered as he came up to her. He looked pleasantly stunned. "Nell. I didn't expect . . ."

She nodded, shrugged. "I know. I . . ." *I don't want you to leave. I've come to try to keep you here.* "I wasn't going to."

He looked at her in that quietly intent way that always made her feel as if he could see right inside her. "Why did you change your mind?"

A surge of cowardice made her say, "I . . . suppose I thought I should see you off. It's to be such a long trip, and—"

"All aboard! The train to Providence and points west departs in two minutes!"

Will looked toward the train, his mouth in a grim line.

Nell said, "You don't want to do this, Will. Shanghai . . . that life . . . You're past all that."

So softly she could barely hear him above the surrounding cacophony, he said, "I can't stay here, Nell. I can't bear it."

"A while back," she found herself saying in a timid voice that didn't sound at all like hers, "you told me you could be persuaded to stay."

With a kiss. Just one. *I won't ask for a second. Ever. I promise. And I'll remain in Boston, and we can go on as before.*

He stared at her, seeming at a loss for words. "You were supposed to have forgotten about that."

"How could I?" She knew she was blushing. She didn't care. She held his gaze even though it seemed to sear right through her.

Will flung the cigarette away and took her arm. He led her through the throng and beneath the overhanging roof of the train station. It was shadowy under the eave, and colder, but they were alone—or at least it felt as if they were. The riotous noise and activity receded as Will drew her against the brick wall, positioning himself between her and the platform as if to shield her from view.

The transition from sharp sunlight to dimness was blinding; Nell could barely make out Will's face in the dusky form looming over her. He removed his hat, his gaze fixed on her.

She shivered all over, blood roaring in her ears. Will said her name, but he didn't seem to know what else to say.

Nell breathed in the familiar, comforting scents of clean wool, Bay Rum, and tobacco. She laid a gloved hand on Will's chest, rising and falling so rapidly one would think he'd just sprinted a mile.

His throat moved.

She looked up at his mouth. He was too tall. Even on tiptoe, she'd never reach it.

"All aboard! Last call!"

Will lowered his head a bit, his eyes huge in the dark.

Nell lifted her hands to his shoulders. Still holding his hat, he curled his other hand around her waist and dipped his head farther still.

She whimpered at the hot, soft shock of his lips against

hers. He gathered her in his arms; his hat fell to the ground. Her heart pounded against her stays as he deepened the kiss. A sort of helpless little growl rose from his throat.

This was happening, it was really happening, and it was so much more than she'd thought it would be. It was the earth opening up beneath her, and her falling and spinning as she grappled for purchase. It was delirious; it was shattering.

"Nell . . ." he breathed against her lips. "Oh, God." He held her tight, his lips grazing the edge of her mouth, her cheek . . .

Nothing would be the same now. Everything would change. Will would remain in Boston, as he'd promised. They would try to resist a second kiss, and then a third, and then . . .

They, inevitably, would become lovers, but in secret, a hidden, adulterous affair, dark and furtive. And when they were found out, as they surely would be, she would lose everything of value to her in this world, except perhaps for him.

Her chest ached as she thought about it; her eyes stung. She would lose her reputation, her livelihood, but worst of all, she would lose Gracie.

"Nell?" Will tilted her face up and wiped a tear away with his thumb, his eyes dark with concern.

"I c-can't . . ."

He cupped her head against his chest, the wool of his coat softly scratchy against her damp cheek. "Shh, it's all right, it's all right . . ."

She shook her head. "I can't . . . I can't ch-choose between . . . between you and—"

"I know," he said in a low, strained voice as he tightened his arms around her. "I know, Nell." She felt his warm breath against her temple, felt the soft brush of his lips. "I wouldn't ask you to. You've—" His voice snagged. It quavered slightly as he said, "You've far more at stake than I. I *am* a selfish cur, but not . . ." He pulled back a bit to look down at her. His cheeks were wet, too. "Not quite that selfish."

The train gave a long, mournful hoot, and then another, as its wheels began to churn. It lumbered forward, grinding and hissing around a bend in the tracks, as onlookers waved and blew kisses.

Nell returned her gaze to Will, who was gazing down at her with the oddest, tenderest little smile. "You must promise me," he said as he tucked her scarf into the neck of her coat, "that you will cover your throat in cold weather while I'm gone. You've always been so blasted careless about that."

"I . . . I promise," she managed.

"Do something for me?" he asked soberly. "Stay here, where I can't see you, until the train's gone."

She nodded, her chin quivering.

Will kissed her forehead, turned, and sprinted toward the train as it picked up speed. His scarf flew off and fluttered onto the granite pavement, but he didn't seem to notice.

He won't make it, Nell thought as he reached toward a grab iron on the bright green wooden caboose. *He waited too long, the train's moving too fast.*

Will seized the iron bar with one hand and the back railing with the other, finding his footing on the cab's rear platform with one long leap. Slumping against the green-painted wall, he raked the hair out of his eyes and looked toward the station, searching the shadows beneath the eave as the train disappeared around the bend.

The Gilded Age mystery series by
P. B. Ryan

**featuring Irish immigrant Nell Sweeney,
governess to the wealthy Hewitt family.**

Murder in a Mill Town

0-425-19715-8
Nominated for the Mary Higgins Clark Award!
When the daughter of a local Irish family disappears, Nell
pledges to help find her. However, for Nell, tracing the path of
the missing woman through the seedy parts of 1868 Boston
just may be the death of her.

Death on Beacon Hill

0-425-20157-0
1869: As governess to the Hewitts, Nell Sweeney belongs to no
particular caste—hers is halfway between her Irish brethren
and the Boston Brahmin. But now a double murder
involves both maid and mistress, and it will take cooperation
by rich and poor alike to solve it.

Available wherever books are sold or at
penguin.com

PC735